TIMESHAFT

STEWART BINT

booktrope

Booktrope Editions

2614 868

Cover Design by Troy Johnson
Edited by Sophie Thomas

Previously self-published 2013

This is a work of fiction. Names, characters, places, brands, media, and incidents are either the product of the author's imagination or are used fictitiously. Any resemblance to similarly named places or to persons living or deceased is unintentional.

PRINT ISBN 978-1-5137-0688-7
EPUB ISBN 978-1-5137-0789-1
Library of Congress Control Number: 2016900060

ALSO BY STEWART BINT, AND
PUBLISHED BY BOOKTROPE

IN SHADOWS WAITING (2015)

Acknowledgments

Many thanks to my Booktrope team for their hard work and dedication:

Book Manager and Marketing Manager: Majanka Verstraete

Editor: Sophie Thomas

Cover Designer: Troy Johnson

Proofreader: Michael-Israel Jarvis

And thanks to my good friend, fellow novelist DM Cain, for her unstinting enthusiasm and encouragement

Special thanks to my wife, Sue, son, Chris, and daughter, Charlotte.

CONTENTS

For my good friends Pam and Stan Steer.

PROLOGUE

A CHRISTMAS BABY

25 DECEMBER 1627

Feeling faint. The pain…coming in waves now.

Want to cry out. Frightened.

Deep breaths. That's what he told me, deep breaths. I'll try.

Ooowwww. That spasm's left me drained.

"Doctor, help me, please."

That contraction came sooner than expected. Shivery now. Nauseous. Feel sick.

Contraction more intense. Strange feeling of finality now it's fading. Perhaps it's the last one.

Ooowwww. It wasn't the last one. When's this going to end?

Pain's every minute now. That must mean something.

"Doctor. DOCTOR!"

Groaning again. Not with pain now. But with pushing.

What's that voice telling me to do? To push. To push? What do you think I've been doing?

The door's opening. Who's this coming in? Susie. With more water. That's the third bowl the doctor's gotten through.

What's that he's saying now? "It begins." That's good. I think. Isn't it?

The need to push again. The need to scream aloud.

Gritting teeth. Muscles tightening. Come on. Come on, get out here NOW!

Suddenly comfortable and reassured.

No…pushing again.

Pressure's eased a bit now.

Coming again. Another wave.

Ooowwww.

That's not me crying. Who's crying?

What's that in the doctor's arms? Small, wrinkled, wet. Tiny form cradled in his arms. Tiny, bloody, crying.

Crying.

My baby's crying.

Welcome to the world, Ashday's Child.

SECTION ONE

WorldSave

CHAPTER 1

MALFUNCTION

HEARING THE FIRST BLEEP of the vidlink, Lloyd Bradman looked up irritably from the 3D holo-image in the corner.

"Right in the middle of *Alpha-Zero* again."

"Why don't you switch it to dormant while the programme's on?" asked his wife, frowning as she tried to listen to the soap opera's leading actor.

"Because the calls may be important."

"They never are," she muttered under her breath.

Bradman swivelled the synthetic hide seat on its single leg and jabbed at one of a dozen buttons indented in the chair arm. The four-hundred-square-millimetre computer interfacing screen on the wall sprang to life, framing the craggy features of Walter Redbrick, the CEO of Australia's leading energy company, Datateknik.

Bradman became instantly alert, and the soap opera's full wrap-around sound died away in response to another jab at the control console.

"Walter, what...?"

"Lloyd!" Now it was Heather Bradman's turn to display irritation. She touched a similar control in her own chair to bring a degree of volume back to the holoprogramme, where a freighter was just blasting off from a space station with a crescendo of noise from its hyperboosted engines.

The face on the vidlink wrinkled in protest at the assault on his ears.

"Lloyd, we've got a situation." Redbrick's voice was loud to combat the holocast. "I need to see you right away."

Bradman shot a laser-sharp glance at his wife as the spacecraft banked away from the revolving satellite and headed on its way to the caletonium mining colony deep in the remote star system of Pegasus Four. It was Bradman's favourite soap; a futuristic story of the Alpha-Zero space station, floating on a major intergalactic flight path, offering sanctuary for weary tourists and freighter pilots. Five evenings a week the overpaid cast could be seen on the 3D holosystems in almost all Darwin homes, playing out their tale of everyday space folk.

A jab at another button paused the live show as his mind snapped to more serious matters now, light years away from such far-fetched escapist nonsense.

"What is it, Walter, what's happened?" He stared deeply at his boss's image, and was sure the slightly overlong, wavy hair was a shade greyer than when they had both left the seafront office that afternoon.

"There's been a malfunction in the main reactor at the Macdonnell Conversion Plant." Redbrick's voice sounded urgent, intense; his face drawn. Bradman sensed he was being let into the news gently; that there was worse to come.

And there was.

"The other reactors went into automatic overdrive to compensate, but the computer didn't realise anything was wrong," Redbrick told him. "Each of the secondary reactors slowly built up to critical level, stealing more and more power from the crippled one, until it ran dry and exploded."

Bradman's silence spoke volumes.

And it was a full ten seconds, which seemed like a lifetime, before Redbrick spoke again. "It sparked off a chain reaction. They went up one after the other. There's nothing left of the site." His voice trailed away helplessly.

Bradman swallowed hard. "Is Alice Springs all right?" The Macdonnell Conversion Plant owed its name to being sited partly underground and partly inside a mountain in the Macdonnell range, 240 miles southwest of Alice Springs in the great Australian outback.

Redbrick nodded. "It's laid waste an area of about 150 square miles, but the town's okay."

"At least that's something. When did it happen?"

"Twenty minutes ago. We've just finished running the telemetry readout. That's how we know what caused it. It's all there, down to the precise second the malfunction occurred in the first reactor and the gradual build-up to critical point in the others." Redbrick's voice was now barely more than a whisper, and despite the powerful air-conditioning in his office the communicator clearly showed rivulets of sweat flowing down his face.

Bradman's jaw dropped limply as he drank in the significance of what he had just learned. "I'm on my way over," he said starkly.

Redbrick nodded silently and broke the connection.

Bradman swivelled away from the blank screen and stared unseeingly at the spacecraft on the frozen holocast.

Heather reached across and squeezed his arm. "It's not your fault, is it, Lloyd—the malfunction?"

A faraway look overtook his eyes, his thoughts elsewhere; trying to piece together what could have possibly gone wrong in what he had believed was a fail-safe operation. Two malfunctions at the same time were inconceivable, yet from what Redbrick had told him there must have been two: the original one in the main reactor—in his mind's eye he traced the link back to the central processing core—then there was the warning system which should have alerted the operators immediately. Even if they had not been watching their systems the audio alarm should have cut in long before the other reactors reached anywhere near critical point.

There was no way such a build-up could go unnoticed. He and two Datateknik engineers had devised the energy conversion process and spent many months perfecting it, installing it and constantly monitoring it.

Unless...and he gave voice to his feelings: "Sabotage."

Heather's eyes widened in horror as her hand, still resting on his arm, closed its grip painfully. "Sabotage?" she whispered. "Do you really think so?"

Bradman pulled his arm away, gingerly rubbing the vivid white spots left by her fingers. "I don't know yet," he snapped. "It's just a thought at the moment."

The venom in his outburst died and he reached gently for his wife's hand. "I'm sorry," he said quietly.

She smiled and nodded. "Don't worry, I understand. You'd better go."

Quickly he rolled down his shirtsleeves, donned a jacket and hurried out of the apartment to the elevator. While he was being whisked down the twenty-eight floors his thoughts went out to the conversion plant's ten late-shift workers; to their wives who would now be widows, and to the children without fathers. All because of a malfunction in his system, a system he had assured everyone was fool-proof and safe.

He walked straight past the commissionaire without hearing the old man's hearty wish that he have a nice evening, turning left out of the apartment block on to the bustling street.

Darkness had begun to take its grip on the evening, and all around him artificial light blazed from aircars and from the sky-scraping apartment blocks in this residential suburb of Darwin. A few metres ahead two drunks hailed a cab and stood watching as it hovered over to them, dropping onto its rubber cushions with a gentle sigh. Bradman gave them a wide berth and broke into a trot once he was past. He arrived at the teleport station hot and breathless, and his voice came in quick uneven gasps as he gave instructions to the computer which then debited his company credit chip for the cost of the journey. There were a few other people hanging around the station, but none of them seemed to him to be the sort who could afford the luxury of teleport travel. A young couple—he put them at about eighteen or nineteen—walked slowly ahead of him, giggling, arm in arm. And an elderly man, carrying a brown bottle and wearing a grey coat which had clearly seen better days, was ambling up the ramp towards the double doors.

Brusquely Bradman pushed past, ignoring the teenagers' abusive comments. There was no time for messing about; he was man in a hurry, a man with a mission. *These people shouldn't be here, anyway*, he thought. *How can they afford to be beamed through a teleport?*

Only one of the doors hissed aside as he strode up to it. He was used to the doors of Station Eight both opening to cope with the rush hour crowd he usually travelled with, wanting to get to Darwin's main business area on the seafront. As usual the stark, clinical whiteness of the empty interior assaulted his eyes momentarily. He thrust his credit chip into the slot for verification that he had, indeed, just given the computer the correct details.

"Station Five, and quickly," he demanded, looking through the opaque panelling into the control centre beyond. "I'm in a hurry."

The operator stared back impassively. "There's a couple more people coming in. I'm sorry, but you'll have to wait for them."

Bradman cast an irritated glance over his shoulder at the teenagers and the old man as they strolled up the ramp. He pressed himself into a corner of the ten-metre teleport booth, hoping they would not try to start a conversation with him. The old man headed for the opposite corner, while the young couple stood in the centre. The girl turned to Bradman.

"This is our first time," she enthused, her eyes bright and shining. "In a teleport, I mean. What's it like?"

What *was* it like—what was the sensation of having a computer unscramble your bodily molecules at a subatomic level, transmit them like an email through the ether, and then reassemble them in (hopefully!) the right sequence by the computer at the destination booth? "Wait and see," muttered Bradman. "It'll be over before you know it, anyway." He looked angrily at the operator through the glass, willing him to beam them away from the city's southern suburban sprawl to Station Five on the northern waterfront.

At last, he thought as the operator's blue-uniformed arm reached out towards the computer keypad.

In the same second that he saw the red transmitter light engage and felt the faint vibration of the teleport booth energising, he became aware of wailing sirens and the operator's colleague yelling: "Malfunction! Don't send them."

But the slight dimming of the lights and the sudden murkiness of the void beyond the glass panel told Bradman it was too late; they had already been sent on their way. The siren died instantly, as did the frantic shouting from the control room. They were miles away by now.

The old man cast Bradman a wary look, but the teenagers seemed untroubled, lost in their own world of wonder, romance and awe. The two pairs of young eyes stared around, seemingly fascinated at the emptiness.

"We're stuck," announced the old man suddenly. "Trapped in the void."

"Stuck? What do you mean?" The girl's voice was getting higher with every word. She gripped her boyfriend's arm.

"It's broken down," said the old man cheerfully. "We could be here for days."

"Shut up," snapped Bradman, seeing the youngsters turn deathly pale. "We've been reassembled here, wherever *here* is. So there's nothing to really worry about. We're in one piece."

"But it's still broken down," said the old man. "We could be here for days and days." He unscrewed the top from his bottle, thrusting the neck into his mouth and taking a deep swig of its contents.

"Ah, that's better," he sighed, wiping the moisture from his lips with the back of a grubby hand. "Oops, sorry, forgetting my manners." He offered the bottle to Bradman who waved it away with a disgusted look. The old man's noble gesture elicited the same response from the teenagers.

"What did you mean when you said we could be stuck here for days?" The girl's voice was quivering, still high-pitched, and Bradman guessed she was on the verge of hysteria. *For God's sake don't let her be claustrophobic*, he found himself thinking.

"Days and days and days," echoed the old man after another gulp from his bottle. He belched, and the strong, sickly scent of sweet cider reached Bradman's nostrils.

"What do you mean?" cried the girl again. Her boyfriend laid his arm protectively around her shoulders, but Bradman felt the young man was probably as much in need of comfort as she was.

"We're stuck here until they can mend it," said the old man.

"How long will that be?" asked the boy, his voice shaky.

"As long as it takes." The old man fastened his bottle and slipped it into the depths of his shabby, grimy overcoat. "But it could take days and days and days."

Bradman stared at the tramp's old, lined face, noting with distaste the small weasel eyes set too close together, the lank grey hair in need of a wash, and the narrow tapering chin desperately in need of a shave.

"Just what do you mean by that?" he demanded. For all that he had used the teleport almost daily for the past fifteen years to commute to his office, along with regular site visits, he had never experienced a breakdown and had no idea how long a repair was likely to take.

Suddenly he felt a great—and somewhat uncharacteristic—surge of pity for the pathetic young couple; their first exciting time being beamed across Darwin had been spoiled. They would probably never want to see the inside of a teleport booth again.

But Bradman kept the bulk of his sympathy for himself. He was having to share time with this disgusting old man. Time when he was needed urgently elsewhere.

The weasel eyes stared back at him in silence.

Bradman was beginning to lose patience. "I asked you a question," he snapped, then promptly took a pace backwards as a rumbling began somewhere in the depths of the cider-pickled stomach, working its way up to become another full-blown belch.

"What time is it?" demanded the old man, patting his stomach, post-belch.

"He wants to know the time!" A note of almost comical exasperation crept into Bradman's voice as he spread his hands helplessly towards the young couple.

"No, please," insisted the old man. "It's important."

Bradman glanced at the digital display screen on his wrist, expecting it to say somewhere between eight and nine o'clock. After all, he had only been out of the apartment about twenty minutes and *Alpha-Zero* was still on the 3D holo when he left.

He stared at his watch in astonishment. Eleven minutes past four! *It can't be.* He glanced up, a frown creasing his brow. Another look. The same. And he noted that the seconds had stopped, too.

"It's stopped. What have you done to my watch?" he shouted angrily, his gut telling him the tramp must somehow be responsible.

Before the old man could respond, the boy chipped in: "Mine's stopped, too. But this can't be right, it says 4:11."

The girl turned her puzzled face towards Bradman. "And mine."

Bradman was beginning to feel out of his depth. All three watches were showing the same time. The same *wrong* time: 4:11 and fifteen seconds. The old man appeared to be doing a calculation in his head, silently mouthing figures while counting off the fingers on his left hand. He raised an arm as Bradman started to speak. "No. Quiet," he ordered. There was a new degree of authority to his voice.

Like a tame lamb Bradman stood mute, waiting obediently for him to finish.

"Right," said the old man eventually. "Sorry about that. Just working something out, you know."

Bradman just had to ask. "What?"

"You were expecting it to be about half past eight, weren't you?" He didn't seem to notice Bradman's limp nod of acknowledgement, but carried straight on. "Your watches say just after four...yes? A difference of four and a half hours, right? So, any time now..." He broke off, extending both arms towards the doors.

Nothing.

"Well?" Bradman asked after a couple of moments.

The old man frowned. "My timing can't be that much out, surely. Ah, here we are."

As he spoke the double doors hissed aside to let daylight flood it. *Daylight*. Bradman thought for a fleeting second that he must be going mad. It had been getting dark outside when they stepped into the teleport. And what were all those people doing outside, just standing there, frozen, like statues? Dozens of people, completely immobile.

"Come on, I've got something to show you." The old man sounded like an excited schoolboy. Bradman didn't protest when he felt his arm being gripped, but simply trotted alongside, with the young couple bringing up the rear.

All around them the city lay in eerie stillness. Except the city wasn't Darwin. Bradman recognised it thanks to the times he had emerged from the teleport on his visits to the Macdonnell Conversion Plant. This was Alice Springs. The busy main street was full of aircars, but they were all frozen in mid-movement, and not a sound reached Bradman's ears apart from their four sets of footsteps.

"What's happened?" he managed to stammer. "It's almost as if...well...as if time's standing still for everyone except us."

The old man rubbed his hands together gleefully. "I'm proud of you, Mr. Bradman, I truly am." Bradman didn't begin to wonder how the old man knew his name. In fact, he did not even notice having been addressed by name, he was too engrossed in wondering about other things. "That's exactly what's happened, Mr. Bradman: the malfunction in the teleport has caused us to remain 'in transit' so to speak, trapped between two stations. At that moment in time we were physically nothing more than particles of concentrated molecules, but we had to materialise somewhere. The calculation as to where is based on the speed we were being transmitted and the distance we were travelling."

Bradman stared at the impossibly frozen world around them. "But this isn't Darwin, it's Alice Springs."

"I don't expect even a world-renowned physicist like yourself to understand the temporal science behind this." The old man sounded somewhat smug, rather like an unpopular lecturer explaining something to a none-too-bright student. "All you need know is that we've flipped backwards to a frozen moment in time shortly after four o'clock this afternoon in Alice Springs."

It was impossible for Bradman to rationalise what he was hearing. "Gone back in time?" he sneered. "Don't talk nonsense. What's really happened to us?"

The old man chuckled to himself. "They never believe it, never. I don't know why I bother to explain."

The young couple were staring up at the sky. Thousands of metres above them a hyperboosted aircraft simply hung in the deep blue.

"You believe me, don't you?" he asked them.

They turned towards him, blank expressions masking their faces.

"Never mind," he said briskly. "It's Mr. Bradman I'm concerned with."

Bradman, too, looked at him blankly. "What have you done to us?"

"What have I done to you...?" The rhetoric was slow and patient—again, like lecturer to student. "I've given you a unique opportunity, Mr. Bradman, that's what I've done to you. I've given you a chance to live a few short hours of your life again, to put matters right. Do you follow me now?"

Suddenly, like a flash of lightning, Bradman was able to grasp the old man's meaning. "I don't know how or why, but, yes, I think I do. I can stop the malfunction at the Macdonnell Conversion Plant."

"Absolutely, Mr. Bradman." The weasel eyes shone, maliciously. "You're a worthwhile pupil indeed. I'm proud to be your mentor."

The old man's sarcastic tone was not lost on Bradman, but he chose to ignore it. "How much time do I have?"

"Until they can figure out what we've done to the teleport."

"How long do you think that'll be?"

"Not until you've completed your task, I can assure you of that."

"But the plant's miles away, in the Macdonnell mountain range."

"Your transport awaits you, sir."

Bradman's eyes followed the old man's outstretched arm, coming to rest on a cab frozen at the roadside. Its door was open and two women had been stopped in time just as they were alighting. The old man gently lifted them out of the way and climbed inside. He slid the equally motionless driver across the seat, then deftly flicked his fingers over the computer console.

"Come on, Mr. Bradman, get in."

As Bradman scrambled into the back he heard the door hiss shut and the engine power up.

"Hey, what about us?" cried the teenaged boy from outside, knocking on the window.

"Don't worry," called the old man. "We'll pick you up on the way back."

Bradman peered out at them as the car rose, before shooting away westwards towards the outback and the still intact Macdonnell mountain range.

*   *   *

The teenagers stared at the aircar until it was nothing more than a tiny dot in the distance, and absolute stillness descended on their world once more.

"Well, I like that," snapped the girl. "What do we do now?"

Her boyfriend gazed around at the surreal sight of Alice Springs frozen in time, the frozen people, the frozen cars, the frozen aircraft. "It's like a photograph. A 3D holograph which we're walking through."

"We'd better not go too far from here," the girl continued. "We don't want to miss our ride home."

Suddenly the boy caught a glimpse of movement out of the corner of his eye. "Hey, there's someone over there."

Before his girlfriend could react he sprinted twenty metres to a narrow alleyway. Three tramps wearing similar filthy coats to the one adorning the old man who had just departed, sat leaning against the wall, apparently frozen in time like everyone and everything else. But a fourth tramp was shuffling his way down the alley.

"Wait a minute," shouted the boy as the shambling figure veered drunkenly to one side and vanished through a door.

The boy was halfway down the alley when he heard a scream from behind him. "Tony, help me!" He whirled round and saw his girlfriend struggling with the other three tramps. Her arms were held firmly while one tramp swiftly injected her in the neck with a power-boosted syringe. Immediately she went limp, and the three men gently laid her on the ground.

"Saralee!" yelled Tony, running back towards them. "What have you done to Saralee?"

The tramps formed a line between Tony and the girl, but that did not stop him. Without even breaking stride he flung himself straight at them. Two of them went down with him while the third managed to squeeze against the wall to avoid the human battering ram.

For all that Tony was young and fit he did not stand a chance against all three, because they were not as derelict as they looked. They seemed to shake off the appearance of stooped, drunken losers in an instant, becoming lithe and strong. In a few seconds they had overpowered him, and one reached nimbly inside his stained and tattered coat for another power-boosted syringe.

"Who are you?" screamed Tony, struggling fiercely, trying to break away from the conquering grip which held him firm. "What are you doing to us?"

The tramp's voice sounded surprisingly young and vibrant. "Don't struggle," he ordered smoothly. "We're not going to hurt you. We're taking you home, that's all."

"Home...but how?" Tony's eyes widened in fear as the syringe hovered perilously close to his neck. The tramp holding it thrust his face close to Tony's. "When you wake up you'll be in the teleport booth and you won't remember a thing about this." He pressed the syringe into Tony's flesh and fired the trigger.

In the second or two before losing consciousness Tony caught a glimpse of the fourth tramp coming back up the alley, pulling off his coat to reveal a dark blue uniform beneath. It was the teleport operator, whom he had last seen in the Darwin control chamber. The man seemed to swim across his fading vision.

"Hurry up," Tony heard him say, the words sounding faint as his senses reeled. "I'm ready to get…"

Then Tony sank into oblivion.

* * *

Bradman stared through the aircar's window at the town lying silent and still as they sped towards the urban boundary and the wilderness beyond. The wilderness of the outback, where the Macdonnell Conversion Plant lay in the heart of the mountain range.

He could scarcely believe what was happening. "Just who are you?" he ventured to ask. "How are you doing all this?"

The old man eased the joystick to manoeuvre the car round a vehicle in front of them suspended both in the air and in time. He glanced back over his shoulder at Bradman sitting in the rear.

"Let's just say I'm utilising forces of nature which you haven't learned to tap yet. And you can think of me as Ashday's Child."

"Who?"

"Enjoy the trip, Mr. Bradman."

"Ashday's Child…but what…?"

"If I were you I'd start thinking how to rectify that malfunction in your reactor." The old man gestured at the statuesque landscape beyond the aircar's windshield. "It may look like it out there, but you haven't really got all the time in the world. You'll have to work fast." He hit a key on the console and a sound-proof sheet of plastiglass slid up smoothly between them, cutting him off from any more questions.

Bradman nestled back in his seat and began to picture the reactor's main circuit board.

But try as he might, concentration continued to elude him. His mind was still reeling from the considerably unlikely events of the day. First, the explosion caused by a malfunction—more likely two malfunctions—in the system he had told everyone was fail-safe; in fact, the number of safety features built into it had become legendary among his fellow Datateknik directors who felt he was being too cautious. And equally unbelievable was what was happening to him now. For a moment or two he seriously considered the possibility that he might be dreaming—that this was all a nightmare. But he could clearly recall all he had done during the day; what he had eaten for lunch and dinner, the appointment he had kept, and the people he had seen. And just before leaving the office he had made his final commitment to Walter Redbrick that the result of a full month's online test operation of the prototype reactor, following its successful month's offline simulation, would be ready within two days. No, he had definitely not been dreaming that. So had he fallen asleep watching *Alpha-Zero*? He was confident he had not. He stared hard through the plastiglass at the back of the old man's head, noting how the straggly grey hair hung in greasy strands over his collar.

Again he looked outside. The sprawl of civilisation thinned as the aircar raced towards the southwestern border of Alice Springs. Within moments they were flying over the desolate brushland, the spread of buildings behind them no more than shrinking dots on the horizon.

Eventually they reached the outer rim of the Macdonnell range, where the barren, flat terrain began to bulge into hills and mountains. Bradman had made this trip many times, but never in such bizarre circumstances. It still defied belief that beyond the confines of the aircar the whole world was apparently frozen in time, and that he was on his way to prevent a cataclysmic explosion that had already happened. But no, it *hadn't* happened, had it? Not yet? At least not in this particular moment in time, four hours into his past. And yet, in his own present, it had. Forcing those inexplicable paradoxes to the back of his mind he summoned every ounce of willpower he had to bring his thoughts under control.

The reactor. What caused the reactor to break down, and why did the monitoring system not alert the operators? *A self-diagnostic run on the computer would be the quickest way of pinpointing what needs to be done,* he thought to himself. *But even that will take some time. Are there any other ways of doing it?*

Under the expert control of the elderly tramp the aircar wound its way unerringly between the bases of several mountains until it came to Solar Peak—the unofficial name given to it by the Datateknik team working thousands of metres below it. The vehicle climbed to a flat ledge about one hundred metres up, then sank onto its cushioned supports with a hydraulic hiss. The old man touched two buttons to open the front and rear doors, and climbed out.

Bradman alighted, too. His companion pointed to a small slot in the rock face. "I believe I need you for this," he said amiably. Seen up close, it was almost as if a giant knife had scored a mathematically perfect three-metre square in the face of the mountain.

"Yes." Bradman's voice positively dripped sarcasm. "I'll open the door for you." For a second or two he stood looking out across the desolate landscape. Nothing moved. Indeed, there was nothing there *to* move.

The tramp pulled up a sleeve and made an exaggerated show of looking at his watch. There was something about that simple action that rang warning bells for Bradman, but for the life of him he could not put his finger on it.

"Mr. Bradman, please..." It seemed the old man was becoming increasingly worried about rectifying the problem in time.

"Are you able to help me find the fault?" asked Bradman. "I could do with some assistance once we get inside. It'll be quicker if we're both working on it."

The old man shook his head. "Regrettably not. If I could, I wouldn't need to bring you here, would I? I would do it myself, but sadly I don't have enough working knowledge of your process. You're the expert, and I'm told you're the only one who can possibly carry this off."

Bradman cast him a cynical glance before pushing his company ID chip into the slot. Immediately a small horizontal section of rock, roughly the size of Bradman's i-tablet, extended out from the rock face to reveal an opaque scanning screen. Bradman then pressed the palm of his right hand on to it, activating the computer's voice circuits.

"Access time: 4:11 and fifteen seconds, July 30, year 2345." The computer had been programmed with a soft female voice of neutral accent. "Access security code oh-one-eight-five-two-oh-nine-two.

Personnel: Bradman, Lloyd Timothy Michael. Status: Datateknik Energy Director. Handprint verified. Access granted."

With a gentle electronic buzz, the three-metre square slid smoothly aside, revealing a stark white corridor illuminated by concealed ceiling lights.

Once they were inside the door hissed shut, and the only sound was the hollow tap of their footsteps on the metallic floor as Bradman led the way to an elevator door. "Down to the eighty-seventh level," he said, gesturing for the old man to go through.

Bradman was hoping there would be enough time for the control computer to run its full self-diagnostic program, when the old man's question cut in on his thoughts. "I'm told your energy conversion process is a spectacular concept. How did you come across it?"

Bradman loved talking about his favourite subject—particularly his role in devising the current experimental reactor system—but he could only speak of it in the right circles. One of the reasons the project was tucked away deep underground and in the heart of a mountain in the Australian outback, was that it was still very much at the classified stage. Only a handful of very senior government officials were aware of its existence. And Bradman knew that when it became public knowledge there would be a vociferous protest from the solar and hydrogen power industries. But, of course, if his mission in preventing the coming tragedy should fail, the whole world would know about it in a matter of hours, which would spell the end for Datateknik's revolutionary solar wind conversion scheme. And this unsavoury man *was* helping him, so what harm could it do to skirt around the edges a little?

He glanced at the indicator to check the elevator's progress. Just a few seconds more to the eighty-seventh.

"Well, what we do is convert the solar wind into a form of almost limitless power," he began.

"I thought we already had that resource, Mr. Bradman."

"I beg your pardon?"

"We've been using solar cells to convert sunlight directly into electricity for three hundred years. What's so special about your process?"

"*Sunlight*, yes. That's been powering many homes and businesses for centuries through individual semi-conductors, and most satellites currently orbiting the earth draw on sunlight for their power. The raw energy the earth gets from the sun is mainly light and various forms of electromagnetic radiation which is used to generate heat or electricity. But the particular type of solar cell needed to utilise it is still too inefficient and expensive to be used commercially."

Almost imperceptibly the elevator ended its descent to level eighty-seven, many thousands of metres underground. The door sighed open and Bradman stepped out, indicating that they should turn right.

"The solar wind, however, is a totally different matter. A stream of charged particles originates in the sun's corona, and is ejected from the upper atmosphere. But this wind is highly unstable. Direction and speed vary considerably, and quite often high speed winds hit those travelling slower. These wind speed variations buffet the earth's magnetic field and can produce storms in our magnetosphere."

"Magnetosphere?"

"The magnetosphere acts as a barrier, deflecting the particles around the earth. However, sometimes they're able to penetrate the edge of this region, and can cause radio interference. Occasionally these storms are so severe that they knock out our power grids."

"Is that what caused the worldwide power outage in 2248?"

"Absolutely, and the one that hit Australia in 2250, along with numerous others over the years. But if the solar wind is properly harnessed it can be used on a commercial basis to power the entire world.

"Our project is geared towards channelling and taming the solar wind. We have a number of channelling dishes at the top of this mountain to collect that energy and drop it into a series of underground reactors…"

"Where you convert it into the cheapest form of power mankind has ever had," concluded Ashday's Child. "But what about the cost to the environment? What harm is it doing to the earth?"

"Absolutely none. As well as being the cheapest, it's also the safest, cleanest, and greenest form of energy. Unlimited cheap energy for as long as we want it."

"Are you absolutely sure of that? They had the same high hopes for nuclear energy in the mid-twentieth century. Was it not confidently predicted that nuclear power would usher in a golden age for humanity—the cost of energy would be too cheap to even bother monitoring?"

He's obviously read his history files, mused Bradman to himself. "But what actually happened? There were many accidents involving nuclear meltdown, were there not?" An unpleasant sneer fixed itself on the tramp's face, his eyes holding Bradman's unwaveringly. "You've had your first major accident already and you're not even operational yet."

"Yes, I know. But thanks to your help—however you're doing this—we can correct that fault and ensure it doesn't happen again," said Bradman. "Ah, here we are." They had come to a door at the end of the corridor, which gently slid aside, revealing the reactors' control area. The personnel on the day shift were all eerily immobile at their stations, and again Bradman found himself wondering how the malfunction, whatever it was, had failed to be picked up.

He eased a frozen scientist away from his post at the telemetry monitor and sat down, hitting the key to return the computer to its start-up screen. Using a combination of the keyboard's touchpad and the on-screen icons he flicked through the launch sequence for the main reactor's systems diagnostic, noting with a sinking feeling that the full run would take around forty minutes.

Hovering somewhat menacingly in the background, the old man was constantly checking his watch, becoming increasingly agitated. A fleeting thought flashed through Bradman's mind that back in the teleport booth Ashday's Child had asked him the time. And that was what had gnawed away at him when they stood on the entrance ledge earlier. *Why would he ask me the time when he's got a watch himself?* The thought dissipated as he returned his attention to the computer.

The diagnostic unearthed a few minor systems errors which it repaired automatically, but the minutes specially given by this enigmatic figure outside the normal flow of time, ticked away relentlessly…until:

"Here it is," cried Bradman, pointing to the computer screen and pausing the diagnostic scan. "A cracked control rod."

Then his face fell. "We don't keep any replacements on site. We've never had a problem with the rods before. I'll have to go back to Darwin to get a new one."

Again there was a glance at the watch, and Ashday's Child shook his head. "No, Mr. Bradman, you're asking too much now. You don't have time to replace it."

"Then why the hell did you bring me here?" shouted Bradman. "I thought I was coming to fix the problem, to prevent the explosion." He sank back into the seat, defeated. "If I can't replace the rod I can't stop the disaster."

"But you can."

"I *can't*. Don't you understand? This rod is what caused the chain reaction. It's cracked and I can't mend it. I must replace it."

"Not necessarily." The tramp reached into the seemingly endless depths of his overcoat to retrieve the sweet cider. "Is there no other way to stop the reactors reaching a critical overload?" he asked, taking a generous swig, swallowing deeply and savouring the sweet liquid.

"No, of course not." Suddenly realisation dawned. "Except…the warning system."

Ashday's Child secreted the bottle away in the folds of his coat once again. As before, after emerging from the teleport booth, he rubbed his hands gleefully and a patronising tone entered his voice. "Of course, Mr. Bradman. I am truly proud to be your mentor. What you must do is ensure that the warning system's functioning properly, make the operators realise something's wrong. If they know that, they can prevent the explosions, can't they?"

Bradman's eyes gleamed. "Yes, indeed, and there shouldn't be a problem with that, either. If the circuit's faulty there are plenty more here which I can put in. We do keep those on site."

A sudden repeated clicking drew his attention to the neighbouring computer. Its screen had begun scrolling programming language: its hard drive was being accessed. In a flash he leapt across to it, but his frantic keying had no visible effect.

"Someone's downloading our systems files. But how could they get in?"

Yet another look at the watch. "Mr. Bradman, I strongly suggest we concentrate on the matter in hand. I don't know how long we've got before the teleport is repaired and we emerge on the Darwin harbour front about five hours in this particular moment's future."

"But someone's stealing my work!"

"If you don't succeed in correcting this malfunction there won't be any secrets left to steal," said the tramp. "Let's ensure the warning system's working properly first, then we'll look at this."

Bradman shot another look at the screen where the stream of information was flowing into someone else's memory banks. Reluctantly he nodded and moved back to the telemetry screen, resuming the scan.

"I really don't think we have time to complete the diagnostic scan," commented Ashday's Child. "Don't forget, Mr. Bradman, that we're trying to prevent a disaster that has already happened. I'm helping you change the course of history. Do you realise what an astonishing phenomenon that is? I think we can afford to skip some of the niceties—some of the details—don't you? We know that the system must be down somewhere or the operators would have picked up on the cracked rod. Why not just replace the warning circuits?"

Bradman considered the situation. "The warning fault might not have happened yet, anyway...not at this particular moment in time. The alarm wouldn't be raised until the reactor levels reach amber, which would still give them plenty of time to bring in a new rod from Darwin. Yes, changing the circuits now will work." He started to move across the room towards the main reactor computer, but found his arm in a vice-like grip.

"While you're doing that, is there anything I can do to try to stop this hacker?" The tramp lowered his eyes a fraction, and Bradman noticed how shifty he had become. "I must admit I'm a little intrigued that someone's managed to access this little time bubble I've created. If I can trace the source using your access codes, perhaps we may be able to stop him." Then, quietly musing more to himself than to Lloyd Bradman: "Not long now. It's easier than I thought it would be."

Suddenly he became aware of Bradman speaking to him again, handing him an infochip.

"Sorry?"

"I said, this infochip will run my access codes for the systems computer," repeated Bradman. "If you reload them using the same file pathways they should lock on to the hacker's route and you may get into his computer."

The old man took the infochip and inserted it into the port, initially following loading instructions on the screen—but he merely pretended to run the program. He glanced across at the main reactor computer where Bradman had unclipped a panel in the processing motherboard and removed the central warning core.

"No sign of any wear or loose circuit wires," the scientist told him.

Bradman's infochip disappeared into the voluminous interior of the tramp's grimy coat. "It must malfunction sometime in the next hour, though," said Ashday's Child. "Get the new one in quickly, before the teleport's fixed and we're whisked out of this time bubble back to your own present."

"Right. The new ones are over here." Bradman started to hurry towards a storage area, but again found his arm tightly gripped.

"Just a moment, Mr. Bradman. Is the computer now completely blind to the malfunction in the reactor?"

"It is, yes." As he spoke, Bradman caught for the first time the evil glint in the weasel eyes and saw, too late, the old man's other hand raised high above his head, before smashing the now empty cider bottle with alarming force on to his exposed temple. As the glass shattered around his ear, Bradman saw stars before falling senseless to the floor.

Standing over him the old man looked down at the jagged stump of the bottle still in his hand. "The old-fashioned ways are always the best," he said. "Just as effective as these new-fangled booster syringes."

*   *   *

Bradman winced painfully as the medic gently rubbed ointment into the bruise. "I just don't understand it, Walter."

"Don't worry about it, Lloyd. At least you're okay, although you've got a nasty bruise on your head. You must have been jolted pretty hard against the wall when you finally materialised."

Since recovering consciousness several moments ago Bradman had been trying to get things clear as to what had happened. "How long were we trapped in limbo?" he asked, a little uncertainly.

"Almost three hours," replied Redbrick.

Long enough to have travelled to Macdonnell and disconnected that warning circuit, Bradman thought miserably. Suddenly his addled brain began to see things in a slightly clearer light. "The old man, Ashday's Child. What's happened to the old man?"

A puzzled look creased Redbrick's brow and played at the corners of his mouth. "What old man? Ashday's Child?"

Now it was Bradman's turn for puzzlement. "The old man in the teleport."

Redbrick shook his head. "There wasn't any old man, Lloyd. Just you and two teenagers."

The words stunned Bradman and his head refused to stop spinning. No old man? It did not make any sense. "But he was in there with us," he protested.

Redbrick laid an arm on his shoulder. "Don't worry, Lloyd. It's the bang on the temple that's done it."

"But those teenagers saw him, too. They came to Alice Springs with us."

Redbrick shrugged his shoulders. "We've already spoken to them. They didn't mention any old man—they said there was just you in the teleport with them. And Lloyd, you didn't go to Alice Springs. The teleport malfunctioned just after you left Station Eight. You rematerialised there after it was fixed."

Bradman's mind continued its dizzying whirls. "But the old man...what could have happened to him?" *If he was really there at all.*

"We've spoken to the teleport operator as well." Walter Redbrick's words were as gentle and as soothing as he could make them. "He told us there were just three of you on that trip."

"But the old man was there in the teleport, too," insisted Bradman. "He *was*. He took me on to Macdonnell and..." He broke off in a cold sweat as a terrible thought crossed his mind. "Oh God, no," he gasped, looking at Redbrick in anguish. Brushing the medic's arm aside he pushed himself up onto his elbows. "You told me on the vidlink that the telemetry readout pinpointed the exact time of the reactor's malfunction...?"

Redbrick nodded. "That's right, Lloyd. It seems the main control rod cracked around quarter to four, but there wouldn't have been enough build-up in the other reactors to trigger the warning system until much later. Unfortunately the circuit controlling the warning system malfunctioned as well."

Bradman felt faint and sick. "What time did the safety circuit go offline?" His voice was distant and helpless. He knew the answer already.

"About ten past four, I think."

It had to be more accurate than that. He could still hear the teenage boy saying his watch had stopped at 4:11, and his own incredulity upon realising that everyone's watches had stopped at that same wrong time. It was also the time the computer logged his access to the Macdonnell site. "Do you have the exact minute and seconds?"

Redbrick looked puzzled again. *It's the bang on the head,* he told himself. *Humour him.* He pulled up a file on his i-tablet. "Yes, here we are. 4:11 and fifteen seconds."

CHAPTER 2

THE GRAVE OF JONATHAN ALLMAN

"OI, PHILLIP, STEADY ON." Coming from Kent, famously known as the Garden Of England, Nadia Reeder couldn't in any sense of the word be called a Cockney. Before beginning her four-year astrotemporal physics course at the Central Academy of Greater England, her speech had readily betrayed her London roots, but after listening to, and conversing with, a variety of accents and dialects, her voice had lost much of its native harshness.

More than her voice had changed during the years Phillip Oatridge had known her. He had witnessed the metamorphosis from adolescent orphan who had never known her parents, to a radiant young woman of twenty-three who had thrown off the last lingering remnants of puppy-fat to reveal an athletic and powerful figure which would never be truly slim. The hairstyle was more predictable than it had been once—still long, but now washed every day; the rebellious student days behind her.

Nadia rubbed her elbow gingerly. The timepod had lurched violently at the exact moment she chose to step through the doorway from the compact living quarters into the tiny control area, causing her to stumble sideways, cracking her arm against the jamb.

Phillip could barely afford to acknowledge her presence, let alone find the time to tell her the sudden swaying wasn't his fault. He was too busy trying to decipher the mass of information that suddenly started scrolling down computer screens set into three of the control consoles facing the two pilot seats. He punched key after key, then peered again at the screens, shaking his head in frustration.

"Very strange," he muttered. "Very strange indeed."

Like Nadia's, the final eighteen months of his astro-temporal physics course had been sponsored by TRAEP—the Time Research and Exploration Project—and on graduating with First Class Honours degrees, both had begun training for TRAEP's inaugural mission: to pilot a timepod to a predetermined position in history.

The timepod was barely larger than an average motorhome of the late 1990s, the era chosen for the vessel's first trip.

"What's happened, Phillip?"

Again the pod lurched, sending Nadia tumbling forward. This time it was her wrist which cracked resoundingly against the edge of the overhanging console. She clung with her other hand to the underside of the panel, praying it wouldn't come open and leave her sprawling on the floor clutching an amputated circuit board.

As the timepod rocked and shook, Phillip's expert gaze continued to scan the computer screens. "Whatever the malfunction is, it's a strong one."

"Can we fight it?" Nadia asked as she slipped into her co-pilot's seat.

Phillip pulled his joystick from its neutral position. "We'll have to switch to manual and set down somewhere," he said, jabbing at three red keys in quick succession, to take control from the computer's pre-set co-ordinates. Almost instantaneously the screens stopped their frantic scrolling as the errant vessel appeared to stabilise.

But the smoother passage was gone in a second, as, freed from its computerised locks, the pod began to yaw dangerously.

After Nadia released her joystick from its neutral holding bay, it took her several pounding heartbeats to match his controls, but when they were finally synchronised, the pod's unruly swinging started to subside.

Their hands darted across the instrumentation almost as if belonging to one entity, slotting home key after key, powering up for a manual landing. The milky white mist beyond the front observation port showed no trace that anything was different from a few moments earlier, but the computer told an altogether different story. A massive power surge had caught the craft, dragging it off course. The computer wasn't able to compensate because the pod had been carried too far beyond its pre-set parameters and was being buffeted by time currents.

Expert handling by the two pilots recovered a measure of control and the horizon-line indicator levelled out.

"Let's see if we can get down without too much of a bump," said Phillip.

"Sure thing," Nadia replied.

Information being fed automatically from their body monitors into the on-board computer recorded that despite a calm exterior—the result of their intensive training—their physical and mental states were anything but calm. After all, they were in uncharted territory. Heartbeats raced, blood pressure increased, even kidney, liver, and spleen functions were acting irrationally.

They barely noticed the ever-present vibrating background hum increasing in pitch a fraction as they brought a variety of circuits into play, while cutting others.

Any living being who happened to be in the immediate vicinity of the landing site would have noticed a slight whoosh of wind at first as molecules of air were pushed aside, making room for the pod's entry from another dimension. At first the landscape was still; the next a grey motorhome-sized vessel slowly faded into existence. Inside, as it solidified, the humming of its power supply slowly diminished until the landing sequence was complete. The timepod had made its first journey. Not the one planned for it, but nevertheless, it had successfully come to rest centuries from its starting point.

Nadia ran her fingers over the navigation controls. "Let's see where we are," she said. Then, looking across at Phillip she raised her eyebrows. "Or should I say *when* we are?"

Phillip was already peering through the front port, taking in the country scene of young saplings planted close to each other. "Okay," he said. "You check the 'when' and I'll see what's out there."

He touched a switch that lifted a video camera through a small roof hatch, relaying video images to one of the computer screens. Another control pushed the camera's range further through the thicket, but its searching eye only picked out even more trees. The pod appeared to have settled on a dry, rutted path in the middle of a recently planted wood.

"The seventeenth century, I think," murmured Nadia. "I can't be sure, though. We've been pushed well off course. It'll take me a while to calibrate the parameters and get an accurate computation."

She glanced up at Phillip, then turned to look through the window. What she saw caused her to shout in alarm.

"I see it too, Nadia." Phillip's beetling brows pulled even further down.

"What is it?"

"I don't know."

The movement seemed to be affecting everything outside. The dozens of oaks and sycamores within sight were all changing. The video camera's zoom showed the same thing was happening further away. Light and shade alternated like a strobing screen; leaves withered on the branches and fell to Earth, replaced by budding new shoots almost in the winking of an eye. Like a film sped up many hundreds of times the seasons flashed by beyond the window and on the screen; the trees growing taller and more dense, swiftly becoming covered with snow, bathed in bright sunlight, then whitened out with snow again, before everything became too much of a blur to see any more.

Phillip studied another instrument display. "We've ended the landing sequence. The pod's down properly, yet we're still moving through time. Not space—we're fixed in one physical spot, but we're moving forward in time."

Even as he spoke, the blur on the screen and through the port began to slow into shapes they could again make out more readily. Some of the trees had disappeared, while others were now fully mature and hundreds of years old. About a mile in the distance the video's enhanced image showed a large stone house with a long, straight driveway leading to it through towering wrought-iron gates. A massive oak front door graced the top of a sweep of steps, with four windows on either side. The first floor had nine windows on the front elevation, completing the opulent grandeur.

Phillip adjusted the camera's depth control, but before either of them could take in any more detail of the building's splendour, time speeded up again, whisking three bulldozers out of thin air to crush the now ageing and suddenly derelict house to the ground. And all the while, a small church which stood a few hundred metres from the house, remained intact. Its stonework, and, latterly as time sped by, some brick repairs, darkened through weathering and age. Several name plates came and went with the passing years which, to

Phillip and Nadia, had become half minutes each, but they all read the same: St. Dunstan's.

The graveyard on three sides of the church inched its way further out, and the early tombstones faded and aged in front of their eyes. Weddings alternated with funeral services in the span of a breath, and Nadia found herself wondering how many of those funerals were for the happy couples she caught a glimpse of rushing in and out of the church.

People's whole lives passing before her eyes; *entire centuries, countless generations, must have come and gone in the few moments we've been here,* she thought.

"Few moments," she said aloud. "That's a laugh. We must have been here for hundreds of years."

"I beg your pardon?"

"Sorry...just thinking aloud." She turned her attention back to the temporal navigation figures. "Hmmm, centuries are just slipping past us. I don't understand it."

Phillip pointed to the video images. "Look at that."

The three bulldozers had returned, but this time in reverse, as the flattened house put itself back together. Tombstones in the now shrinking graveyard alongside the church disappeared, letting their occupants live their lives again from the grave to the cradle and back to their mothers' wombs. The aged trees shrank back into saplings, and for a second or two the land was clear, before growing into the thickly wooded area once again.

Then a few moments later the bulldozers were back, demolishing the house for a second time.

"We must be bouncing backwards and forwards through time. Whatever's going on?"

Nadia shook her head grimly, the only answer she could give.

"We're slowing down again." Phillip was looking from the screen to the port and back again. At last the sun hung motionless in the sky, no longer arcing through the heavens' mixture of blue, black, and grey. The video picked up two men coming into view around the side of the church, one about three inches short of the six foot mark and in his mid-thirties, the other slightly shorter and about twenty-five years older, with a pronounced middle-aged spread. A woman, just under five foot, but looking taller due to the blue high heels she wore with denim jeans and red anorak, pushed a tartan pram through the gateway in the church wall and headed towards the men.

"They're moving at normal speed," said Nadia. "I think we must have stopped." A glance at her computer display showed that they had indeed stopped their erratic time-bouncing. Scanning the controls and computer data, Phillip saw that the engines had successfully powered down and he cut all systems except life support.

While he was doing that, Nadia made some more computations. "We may have originally landed in the seventeenth century, but we're definitely not there now. We're somewhere in the late twentieth century, probably not too many years from our planned destination."

"Let's take a look around." Phillip swivelled his chair and headed towards the outer door, hitting a switch alongside it. With a gentle hiss of compressed air the door slid into its recess, letting bright sunlight flood into the interior of the timepod. Before stepping through, he paused to look back at Nadia shutting down her navigation systems.

Scooping up her time placement recorder which she hoped would be able to pinpoint their exact location in time and space using features of the physical geography near their landing site, she followed Phillip outside. He was already hacking with a tree branch at a thicket of brambles barring his path towards the church, as she turned to survey their surroundings.

The timepod stood on a little hillock, really no more than a mound of earth at the edge of an overgrown area measuring about fifty square metres, enclosed within a barbed wire fence.

On the other side of the fence a few hundred metres of grassland separated their landing site from the churchyard. All around them lay playing fields with several sets of goalposts marking the ends of soccer pitches. One set was slightly askew, as if part of a visiting team had spent their time trying to push it over instead of kicking a ball through it. Away to Nadia's right, half hidden by a dilapidated fence and length of bushes, lay an expanse of brick buildings, some two storeys high, some three, some with sloping roofs, some flat.

The persistent drone of engines assaulted her ears, and turning the opposite way she caught a glimpse of fast-moving four-wheeled vehicles beyond the jumble of trees and other greenery. Her extensive knowledge of history told her these were twentieth century automobiles and lorries. And there were lots of them.

A sudden roaring from overhead startled her. A low-flying aircraft came into view above the trees, climbing sharply towards the wispy clouds. The plane was so low she could have read its registration number had she been so minded.

When she looked back to the land Phillip had carved an opening in the thicket and was now attacking the barbed wire. By the time she reached him, the wire was nothing but a tangled mass on the ground, which they stepped over together, heading across the grass towards the church.

"What do you think?" Phillip asked her.

She paused to enter *St. Dunstan's Church* into the time placement recorder, along with other estimated data of their possible whereabouts.

"Possibly London, Old England, late twentieth century." Suddenly a thought struck her, and she turned her gaze to the skies once more, her finger tracing the path the aircraft had taken. "If it is, any minute now there'll be another…" Her words were drowned out by the very object whose presence she was on the verge of forecasting. Another aircraft rose into sight above the trees taking the identical flight path of its predecessor, almost as if they were playing tag.

"Heathrow Airport," she muttered.

Phillip turned to her in amazement. Back home in the twenty-sixth century, TRAEP's sprawling operation was on the site of the former Heathrow Airport. "We set off from somewhere round here, then," he said.

"Six hundred years away, but somewhere round here, yes," laughed Nadia. She looked down at the recorder's screen. "And the computer says…that direction." She pointed towards a mass of buildings beyond the edge of the park.

The woman with the baby in the pram glanced up at them as they made their way into the churchyard, where the younger of the two men was examining a brass plaque set into the wall.

"Here it is," he called to his older companion who was studying plaques on another wall. "Tony Hancock's memorial."

"I know that name," whispered Nadia as she trekked in Phillip's footsteps among the graves. "Tony Hancock? Now where've I heard of him before?" She entered the name into the time placement recorder, cross-referencing it with St. Dunstan's Church. In a few seconds it had accessed the timepod's computer and the answer was flashed to the screen.

"Of course," said Nadia, reading from the visual display. "'One of Old England's foremost comedians during the early era of television, when it was still in its cathode-ray tube phase. Committed suicide in Australia in 1968. His ashes were flown back to the UK and scattered at St. Dunstan's Church in Cranford Park, near Heathrow Airport.'"

As Phillip turned to examine the wording on a couple of tombstones, the elder of the two men was threading his way between the graves, eager to look at his comrade's find.

"I knew it was here somewhere," the man called.

Nadia looked around at the dates on the stones nearest to her. Some were fading and difficult to read, others were much clearer. On one she could just make out 1727, but the elements had smoothed away much of the stonemason's work in regard as to who lay buried beneath it. Another said 1979, and the date of birth was only 1973.

"Caroline Richards," read Nadia. "Poor little thing was only six."

"Here's an interesting one," called the woman with the pram, and Nadia found herself looking up, about to reply, when she realised the intended targets for the comment were the two men and not her.

"A married couple died on the same day as each other," the young mother continued, peering down at the mildewed lettering on a weather-beaten stone.

Nadia wandered alongside her. "How romantic," she murmured. The woman looked up at her and smiled.

Nadia returned the smile, noticing how the woman's eyebrows raised as she took in the silver-grey flight suit and boots. Then she heard a faint muttering coming from the pram. The mother adjusted the covers allowing Nadia to catch sight of a tiny grinning face with the largest, darkest eyes she had ever seen.

"He's gorgeous, what's his name?"

"Christopher." The mother's London accent wasn't as pronounced as the older man's.

"How old is he?"

"Just over four months."

Nadia reached into the pram and flattened the covers which were pulled up to Christopher's chin. *The little button nose and toothless mouth are so cute,* she thought. Christopher looked up into her eyes, giggling.

Nadia smiled at the mother, a raft of emotion running fleetingly across her mind. A mother and child, the most natural relationship in the world. But one denied to her. She had never known either of her parents. She recalled the stories she was told by her adoptive family while growing up; the stories of how her mother died in childbirth, and how her father was killed in a freak accident shortly afterwards.

She turned her attention back to the grave.

Jonathan Allman, she read silently. *A trusted friend, died tragically on June 10 1649. Beloved husband of Louise.* And carved beneath that: *Louise Allman, died of a broken heart June 10 1649.*

"Isn't it sad, Phillip?" she said, pointing to the headstone. "Sad, and yet beautiful at the same time. I wonder how old they were. It doesn't say."

Silently Phillip gazed down at the stonework, the only earthly reminder of a couple who had lived more than three hundred years before the moment in time he and Nadia now occupied, and almost an entire millennium before the world he called his home.

Nadia's attention was suddenly caught by a rustling in a tree above their heads, and she squealed in delight. "Look, Phillip."

His eyes followed an imaginary extension of her pointing finger, coming to rest on a small grey animal scampering nimbly along a branch.

"A squirrel," she gasped. "They've been extinct for over 350 years." With an almighty bound it leapt about five feet on to the church roof and scurried up the slates to disappear over the top, no doubt its sharp eyes already picking out another tree to use as a bridge.

A light breeze disturbed the yew tree next to the grave of Jonathan Allman. Behind Phillip and Nadia the young woman with the pram appeared to start walking backwards away from the two men.

Meanwhile, the squirrel came arcing backwards from the church roof to reclaim its footing on the branch.

CHAPTER 3

Opening Circles

ASHDAY'S CHILD DID FOUR THINGS in quick succession: he tightened his dressing gown cord; settled into the hotel bedroom's easy chair; glanced again at the date on his newspaper's masthead—Thursday, 20 October 1994—and looked at one particular headline: "Poisonous Blow to TCR."

He smiled as he went on to read the story under the byline of the paper's environment correspondent:

"The Austrian Reigning Court has ruled that a leading global environmental group is entitled to call TCR plastic an environmental poison.

"TCR (Tyalide Coryalotaine Rasilate) has come under systematic attack around the world for several years, but this is the first time that a legal ruling has allowed its many detractors to go so far.

"The court ruled against an appeal by three Austrian companies seeking to stop the environmental protection group Sustain from describing TCR as an environmental poison. The judgement found that under certain conditions TCR's principal component, Rasi-Bisolate, can pose hazards to human and animal life, and that in cases of 'improper handling' or in an accident, potential dangers could arise from TCR.

"Therefore, the court ruled Sustain is justified in using the expression 'environmental poison.'

"Byron Thraves, director of TCR's international trade association, the World Council of Bisolate Manufacturers, insisted that the verdict did nothing to undermine TCR's role as a safe and important product, which, in normal usage, has no damaging effects on people or the environment. But he admitted the ruling was 'disappointing,' and could pose difficulties.

"Sustain spokesman Alan Delahay-Ride described the verdict as a 'sensible outcome,' and a step closer to outlawing not only TCR but the whole of the Rasi-Bisolate chemical industry.

"'It is only by such action that the world will become a better and safer place for us all,' he said. 'We live for the day when these two poisons, Rasi-Bisolate and TCR, will be a thing of the past. And that day is not too far away.'

"TCR has been attacked on four main counts: the health hazard to workers during its manufacture; concern over additives; the formation of highly dangerous dioxins in its manufacture and disposal; and difficulties in recycling TCR products.

"The plastic has survived because there is no suitable replacement. TCR is highly versatile, with many applications in the automotive, aerospace, and construction industries."

"Well, TCR won't be a problem for the world much longer," Ashday's Child said to himself. "The ball's rolling now."

A knock on the door interrupted his thoughts. "Come," he called.

"Not dressed yet?" rebuked Caitlin Lang, eyeing his dressing gown as she stepped into the room. "I had breakfast half an hour ago."

Ashday's Child peered at her black leather skirt—which in his opinion was hardly more than an elongated belt—and black leggings. "I'd rather keep my dressing gown on all day than go around looking like that," he said drily. "Anyway this is sustenance enough for me." He threw the paper over to her. "The work we've done in Austria these last few days has made the news."

Caitlin read through the report. "That's great. I didn't think this would get much coverage outside Austria."

"Neither did I. It's a tremendous boost, though. I reckon it's probably brought our campaign forward by about three years. Reuben was on the phone last night to say it's been on television in New Zealand, and there are numerous press reports from all over the world. It's the best gift we could have had."

"From Austria, with love," she mused.

Caitlin was a relatively new recruit to WorldSave, the foremost environmental protection group of twenty-eighth-century Earth, and she relished the opportunity for such timehops, which were made all the more exciting by working with an old warhorse like her current colleague.

Along with many at WorldSave she often wondered about the enigma that was Ashday's Child: who was he; where did he really come from; why did he constantly refuse promotion to a safe desk job as a strategic planner, choosing to remain a field operative; risking injury, or even death, on an almost daily basis during his missions?

He was, without doubt, WorldSave's best agent. *But you'd never know it by looking at him,* she thought, trying not to stare at the close-set, piercing eyes, which just three weeks ago had so unnerved Lloyd Bradman 350 years into this particular moment's future. She felt particularly proud to have been chosen to accompany him on that mission as his assistant and shuttle operator, taking Ashday's Child through the Timeshaft.

To have played a part in what was described to her as WorldSave's most important and telling mission would stay with her to the end of her days. It had been explained to her why they had to create the Timeshaft in 2345, which would stretch from the beginning of time through to the very end of time, enabling anyone entering it to get out on any date they chose.

But the astro-temporal physics behind why they had to create something that was already there, was still beyond her non-scientific mind. "WorldSave's been using the Timeshaft for nearly fifty years," she had protested during the mission briefing. "It already exists, so why do we have to go back to 2345 to create it?"

Before the commander could reply, Ashday's Child had peered at Caitlin over the top of the glasses which he always, but only, wore at WorldSave headquarters. "Because if we don't create it, it simply won't exist," he said patiently. "Meaning we wouldn't be able to go backwards and forwards in time. And if we couldn't do that, those fools who call what they're doing to this earth of ours *progress* would have destroyed the planet long ago—as you well know."

She did, indeed, know that. She knew, for instance, that had WorldSave not gone back more than seven hundred years to instil the break-up of the old Soviet Union, nuclear war would have wiped out two-thirds of the Earth's population and rendered much of the landmass uninhabitable for thousands of years. And she had learned in one of her first training sessions as a field operative that an alternative timeline showed a similar fate would have befallen the planet had WorldSave not engineered the assassination of a United States president in 1963. Also, the rise of North Korea as a world nuclear power had had to be stopped, as had the use of the internal combustion engine, CFC gasses—the list seemed endless.

Would all those good works simply cease to exist if their mission to create the Timeshaft in 2345 were not successful? she had wondered, floored by Ashday's Child's infuriating logic.

"But those things *did* all happen," he had told her. "As you say, we've used the Timeshaft for fifty years, so we know we must have successfully created it in 2345. All we've got to do now is use the Timeshaft to go back to that date to actually do it."

Her thoughts then wandered even further back, to the induction course she attended after signing WorldSave's lifelong membership and security pledge, when the Timeshaft's existence was revealed to the recruits. Until that moment she had believed she had joined an environmental protection group which campaigned against what it saw as activities that were harmful to the planet. How stunned she was, to learn that WorldSave's principal function was an environmental guerrilla operation, with agents time-hopping throughout history ensuring that Mankind was stopped from devastating the planet.

This mission she was on now, for instance, to force the plastics industry to find a replacement for TCR, and the chemical industry a replacement for Rasi-Bisolate, would be successful within ten years. She and Ashday's Child had just been instrumental in sowing the seeds for it by ensuring the Austrian Reigning Court ruled in Sustain's favour, and it would have been impossible without the Timeshaft.

But never in her wildest dreams had she thought she would play a part, however small, in the Timeshaft's creation, until she was called in for that mission briefing.

There were to be nine of them; Caitlin as the shuttle pilot (an honour, indeed, to pilot Ashday's Child's personal shuttle); Ashday's Child as the operation leader; an agent to operate the teleport in

Darwin; two technicians to freeze the teleport using energy bled from the Timeshaft; and four troubleshooters.

"The purpose of this mission is twofold," the commander had told them. "Firstly, to create the Timeshaft, and second, to destroy the prototype of a dangerous solar wind conversion energy process, which, if allowed to continue, will slowly but inexorably leak an undetectable radiation into the atmosphere, causing a deadly mutation in chlorophyll. The world's plant life would be wiped out within fifty years. And without plant life…"

One of the technicians finished the sentence: "…there's no human life."

"Exactly. Now, as with many of our operations, I'm afraid there will be some acceptable collateral damage. We've looked at several alternative plans, but the only way to successfully accomplish both parts of the mission is to make all the reactors at the conversion complex reach a critical overload, causing a massive explosion."

"But how will that create the Timeshaft?" Caitlin wanted to know. She had learned at her induction course that WorldSave technicians could control the constant two-hundred-billion-megaton energy flow in the shaft, enabling the field agents to travel to any precise point in time, past and future. But none of the sessions mentioned its origins.

"Have you ever heard of ley lines?" asked the commander.

"They're imaginary lines, aren't they? The supposed lines of prehistoric tracks, or something?"

"Not imaginary. They're actually lines of powerful kinetic energy criss-crossing the earth in a mathematically perfect network. There are many places where these ley lines cross, but only two places in the world where as many as twenty converge in one spot. One place is the site of the Macdonnell Solar Wind Conversion Plant in the Australian outback, which is where you're going. The other is in London, Greater England, about three miles from the site of the very first time travel experiments around 2100 years ago.

"Those two points where twenty ley lines converge hold as much latent power as a two-hundred-billion-megaton nuclear explosion. What the blast at Macdonnell does—or rather, did—is to disperse that energy, not in space, but in time. It tore a narrow shaft in the time continuum from the very dawn of pre-history right up to the end of the known universe. At least that's what our computer simulations show; it actually goes too far in both directions for us to send manned shuttles all the way yet."

"But we're nowhere near either Australia or London," protested one of the four troubleshooters. "And yet we can get into the Timeshaft here in Scotland."

"Yes, indeed," said the commander. "This is where the global network comes in. I said that although the Macdonnell Conversion Plant explosion dispersed the energy in time, it didn't disperse it in space. What it did do, however, was disperse it through the kinetic power of the ley lines. So anyone with the right technology can access the Timeshaft from any point on any ley line around the globe. Only WorldSave has the knowledge of how to do that, and it means we can use our station here to send a shuttle along that wave of kinetic energy through the Timeshaft."

"You mentioned the London site of those early time travellers," said Caitlin. "How come they didn't latch on to the shaft, especially as they're so close to a ley line?"

The commander smiled. "Those pioneers didn't know it when they took their first tottering steps across the time barrier," he said, "but they were actually tapping into energy from the Timeshaft to pilot their vessels."

"But shouldn't they be stopped?" asked Caitlin. "Isn't it dangerous that they have knowledge of time travel and access to the shaft? I thought we're the only ones with appropriate time travel technology."

"Stop them...?" laughed Ashday's Child. "No. It was us who gave them the secrets of time travel in the first place."

Caitlin now seemed to hear his voice from two places—one in her thoughts, and one in her ears. "Penny for them?" he was saying, dispersing her memories and snapping her back to her present.

"I beg your pardon?"

"Sorry. An expression from Old England. It means 'what are you thinking about?'"

Caitlin smiled, then realised she was staring hard at him. He stared back with those sinister eyes.

She dropped her gaze and looked away, embarrassed, taking in the surroundings of the Kensington hotel room. "I was just...er...thinking..." she floundered, desperately seeking an answer. "How, er, gullible and uneducated the people of this era are, to let all these dreadful things happen to damage the environment."

"That's why WorldSave has developed along the lines it has. It's truly saved the world on countless occasions. And it isn't just this era where people's ignorance and lethargy prevails. It's the same story throughout history.

"The late twentieth and early twenty-first centuries are always recounted on history disks though, because it was here that serious pollution started. Industrial waste and smog, the hole in the ozone layer, the advent of nuclear power, urban sprawl encroaching on the countryside—you name it, they let it happen. But it doesn't get any better as the centuries go by."

"No, I suppose not." She pulled the net curtain aside and peered at the bustling London street nine storeys below.

"Sad, isn't it?" said Ashday's Child.

"Yes." She spent the next few seconds counting the constant flow of cars. "All these internal combustion engines at any one time, all burning either petroleum or diesel—"

"Your historical knowledge serves you well," he interjected.

"—contributing to the world's first major environmental crisis."

Now it was Ashday's Child's turn to sink into memories. "Fortunately WorldSave was able to prevent the greenhouse effect from taking a stranglehold on the earth's temperature," he recalled. "I spent three years here, 1999, 2000, and 2001, putting things right."

She could only imagine what was going through his mind, but the question was on her lips before she could stem it: "Why do you do it?" Straight away she wanted to bite her tongue; she couldn't believe she had asked such a crass, stupid question.

"Why do I do it...?" He smiled. "Because I can imagine the earth as she finally becomes, despite all our best efforts. Without our work this planet would grow diseased early and die millennia before her time. All I'm doing is playing a small part in preserving the earth for a while longer, enabling billions of people to enjoy a life they otherwise wouldn't have had.

"An alternative timeline projection indicates that without WorldSave's efforts mankind would destroy the earth through dioxin pollution and nuclear radiation before the end of the twenty-second century. The Timeshaft has shown that because of our work, the earth, as we know it, survives well into the fiftieth century. That's something to be proud of. That's why I do it."

Again she stared hard at the enigmatic figure. Trying to understand what was going on behind those impenetrable eyes. *He's seventy if he's a day,* she thought. *How does he manage to keep going the way he does?*

It was almost as if he could read her thoughts: "I've spent a lifetime travelling through the Timeshaft," he told her. "I never thought this would happen to me, but it has—I'm getting old and tired."

"The great Ashday's Child? Never."

He looked her up and down. "I don't know where you get the 'great' from," he said, smiling. "I like to think I've done a good job over the years, but I don't think 'great' comes into it."

"You're the role model for all WorldSave's young recruits," she told him. "We all look up to you. Your exploits through the centuries are legendary. Everyone has a favourite tale to tell about your adventures."

His smile had just a touch of self-indulgence in it. "Well, thank you for saying so. I'm just pleased to have done my bit towards the world's survival, and if I've been inspirational for a new generation of environmentalists, then so much the better."

Caitlin tried to penetrate the inscrutable mask, but she sensed his modesty was real. *To assist him on one mission was wonderful,* she thought. *To be here with him on a second, straight after the first, is incredible.* She knew that many of her colleagues at HQ would give their right arm to be in her position.

One thing still troubled her though, from the mission in 2345. "Can I ask you something?" Her voice was nervous, unsure.

"Of course you can." His voice wasn't unsure; it was rock steady as usual.

"Why wouldn't you let them give Lloyd Bradman any amnethol?"

"Would you have given him some?"

"I thought it was WorldSave policy that anyone who comes into contact with us has their memory of the encounter wiped. And yet you let him go free with the full knowledge of everything that happened with you." Caitlin remembered back three weeks to her role as shuttle pilot on the Macdonnell mission. She had been watching on the scanner when Ashday's Child converged on the shuttle with Lloyd

Bradman slung over his shoulder at the same time as the four troubleshooters arrived with the two teenagers, Tony and Saralee. She hit the button to open the door.

"Amnethol, quickly," said the first troubleshooter, casting off his image as a down-and-out as easily as he divested himself of the grimy coat.

Caitlin was right about the amnethol. It was indeed WorldSave policy to use the drug to erase all memory of contact with field operatives. Two millilitres was enough to deepen the sleep already induced in Tony and Saralee by the anaesthetic given to them in the alleyway while wiping all recollection of everything that happened from the time they stepped into the teleport chamber.

"And him?" The technician pointed to Lloyd Bradman.

Ashday's Child shook his head. "No. Let him keep the memory of what he's done."

The technicians looked at each other in astonishment, then at Caitlin, but everyone remained silent. They knew better than to argue with Ashday's Child.

All through their current mission in London and Austria Caitlin had been bursting to ask why he made such a radical decision, but it was only now that she felt sufficiently comfortable with him. Maybe the fact that he was in his dressing gown made him seem, well, somehow more human to her. He also seemed more relaxed, too, she thought, perhaps because the mission had been completed, apparently successfully.

"Lloyd Bradman will never know the full horror of his invention," Ashday's Child told her. "All he was concerned about was 'progress.' Of all the atrocities perpetrated on this planet in the name of progress across the years, his would have been among the most devastating, if allowed to continue. He would have destroyed mankind. I left him with the memory of having killed innocent people. He knows he was tricked; that the explosion happened because he dismantled the central warning system. He'll have ten people's deaths on his conscience. I think that's punishment enough for someone who would otherwise have destroyed the world, don't you?"

"But he didn't mean to do any harm," protested Caitlin, hardly able to believe she was debating such a moral stance with the great Ashday's Child.

"They never do, or so they say. Yet year after year, century after century, we see the collaboration of scientists and businessmen turning a fast buck in the name of progress. Did the inventor of the internal combustion engine really mean to harm the planet's environment? Of course not. It was done for progress. What about the use of CFC gasses? It made life easier, it was progress, but look what it did to the ozone layer. Look at TCR. It makes life easier for almost everyone in the Western world at this particular time, in one way or another. When it was created no-one thought it would come under such fierce attack. It was praised as a wonderful product."

Ashday's Child threw his arms into the air. "But eventually we all saw the damage it did to the planet." There was a long silence before Ashday's Child finally stood up. "Anyway, enough of this, let's check out and head for home."

The debate was over.

Half an hour later they were walking past the lido alongside the Serpentine in Hyde Park. They passed the restaurant and café, stopping as they moved into the shadow of the Serpentine Bridge which loomed above them.

"Okay, you first," said Ashday's Child. He took a quick look around to make sure they weren't being observed, before pressing a small button on the side of his wristwatch. Instantly a stretch of air, three metres high and two metres wide, began to shimmer in front of them. Caitlin stepped into it, experiencing the normal faint disorientation for a split second as the throb of London traffic was replaced in her ears by an electrical hum. At the same time the large expanse of water which had been just in front of her, disappeared. In its place a spacious and well-lit tunnel stretched from left to right as far as the eye could see. And parked in that tunnel, just ahead, was their gleaming mode of transport: a timeshuttle, roughly the size of an underground railway carriage used by millions of commuters in the city and era they were currently in. But that was where its resemblance to anything in twentieth-century Old England ended. The streamlined craft was windowless, and the only sign of any joints in its sparkling alloy exterior was a three-metre door.

Caitlin turned to look at the shimmering patch she had just walked through, expecting Ashday's Child to be just behind her.

Although a distorted Hyde Park was visible in the waving air, with a glimpse of Knightsbridge in the distance, her companion was nowhere to be seen. She stopped to wait for him.

The mid-morning sun filtered in through the portal, darkened somewhat by the shadow of the bridge. But suddenly even that was extinguished. Outside the corridor there was nothing but blackness — just a tall, rectangular hollow in the shining wall. Before Caitlin could react, the sunlight was back again. She started towards it, but was stopped in her tracks by the darkness reappearing.

"What's happening?" she shouted, unnerved. "Ashday's Child, where are you?"

Then she spotted the chronometer above the portal. If she was unnerved before, she was on the verge of panic now. It had been 10.45 a.m. on Thursday, 20 October 1994 when she stepped into the Timeshaft dimension a few moments ago. But the chronometer now showed 11.27 p.m., Friday, 21 October 1994. Almost in the wink of an eye it changed to 3.10 p.m., Saturday, 22 October, and the world beyond the shimmering portal was light again.

She pressed a button on the side of the timeshuttle to open its door, and, almost falling inside, pushed herself into the pilot's seat and brought the computer online.

"Computer, what's happening?" she asked.

The computer accessed the corridor's monitoring systems before activating its voice circuits. "A temporal distortion in the Timeshaft is disrupting the network," the well-modulated female voice told her. "It is currently in your location, namely the era of twentieth-century London, Old England. The waves are causing a temporary fluctuation of the timestream. They will disperse in four-point-two-seven seconds."

"Computer, how dangerous is the distortion?"

"Distortion is not dangerous at its current low level of nought-point-oh-oh-three-eight percent. However, if molecular imbalance reaches critical level, permanent distortion will occur."

"Computer, what is critical level?"

"Temporal distortion waves now beyond this era, heading through the twenty-first century. Critical level would be reached at sixty-two-point-four-two-three recurring."

"What's going on?" demanded a voice behind her. "How did you get in the shuttle so quickly?"

Swivelling her seat around she saw Ashday's Child framed in the shuttle doorway. Beyond him she could still see through the open portal into the sunshine of Hyde Park. The chronometer above it read 10.45 a.m., Thursday, 20 October 1994.

"There's been a distortion in the shaft," she told him, keying in instructions for the computer to bring up the relevant data. "When I stepped through the portal, time outside fluctuated into the day after tomorrow and back again."

"But I came through right behind you," said Ashday's Child.

"No, you didn't." She pointed to the screen set in the instrument panel. "Look at this."

As he digested the information the computer's voice circuits activated again. "Level two warning. Temporal distortion in the Timeshaft is now approaching this era. Molecular imbalance of four-point-oh-eight. Waves in range in precisely ten seconds."

"They're getting stronger," shouted Ashday's Child. He faced the shimmering Hyde Park beyond the corridor and jabbed the control on his watch to close the portal.

"Get us out of here, fast," he instructed, dropping into a passenger seat behind the pilot area, and fastening his lap belt.

Caitlin closed the shuttle door. "I'll take us out manually," she called over her shoulder, bringing all systems on line and powering up the boosters. "Once we're away I'll set the computer co-ordinates to get us home."

"Don't tell me, just do it. Now!"

"Level three warning." There was no change in the computer's inflection. "Temporal distortion waves increasing in intensity and velocity. Impact now nought-point-two-three-seconds."

The ship's external chronometer flashed from 20 October 1994 to 14 January 1995, then to 28 December 1994 as the undulating waves tossed the shuttle around the Timeshaft like a piece of flotsam.

Caitlin was flung from her seat, one hand reaching ineffectually for the lap belt, the other floundering for the manual controls. Ashday's Child, strapped securely in his seat, stretched forward, attempting to catch her, but had to watch helplessly as she was thrown beyond his grasp, cracking her head against the wall and rolling unconscious towards the rear of the cabin.

"Level six warning." The computer's voice circuits were incapable of changing intonation no matter how urgent the crisis. "Second temporal distortion wave approaching. Impact in five-point-one seconds. Level nine warning. Wave increasing in velocity. Impact now nought-point-two-two-seconds."

The wave struck the helpless shuttle, buffeting it even further along the timeline. Dates flashed by on the chronometer in an incredible blur.

"Level twenty warning. Velocity increasing..."

Ashday's Child realised the shuttle must be riding the crest of the wave like a surfer heading for a foaming shoreline.

"...molecular imbalance increasing. Critical level will be reached in one minute fifty-two-point-eight-five seconds."

In computer terms the pause probably seemed like an eternity while it performed another calculation, brought about by a breach of its safety parameters. But in real time it was no more than a fifth of a second, and certainly not long enough for Ashday's Child to notice. What he did notice, however, was the stark result of its findings, announced with no more emotion than if it were responding to a simple systems check: "Destruction of shuttle imminent."

CHAPTER 4

WITCH HUNTER

PHILLIP AND NADIA stared in amazement as the world around them went crazy. Above, the sun raced through the heavens from west to east, chased by the moon, time and time again. The seasons came and went, or, as Nadia's befuddled mind registered them, went and came. Time was running backwards and they were trapped, helplessly watching as the frost and snow of winter replaced the growth of spring.

The land about them became a blur as the speed of passing time increased rapidly. Then they were no longer standing on the gravel path of the graveyard, but were hurtling head over heels through a star-lit panorama of space. Colours blended, blue became green, green became yellow, yellow became white.

Spinning over and over they tumbled through the years. Nadia occasionally caught a glimpse of movement as people apparently rocketed past, near the house or in the wood. Then, just for a split second, she became aware of solid ground beneath the soles of her silver-grey boots, but that's all it was, just a split second. She felt herself airborne again, but this time her erratic movement almost stilled, was almost dreamlike, as she turned over and over, slowly, slowly. Then, finally, time caught up with itself and as her movements resumed normal speed her momentum carried her forward and she was rolling through a mass of bracken.

Alongside her, Phillip appeared out of thin air. But he, too, was moving slowly. Turning head over heels just feet above the ground, one revolution taking a full thirty seconds. Then, as with Nadia, the slow motion ended, and he somersaulted at full pelt through the same patch of bracken before crashing into a tree with a sickening thud. He groaned, rubbing his legs where they had hit the tree. Nadia scrambled to her feet, looking around, trying to get her bearings.

They were still in the graveyard, and St. Dunstan's Church still stood nearby, but both were changed considerably. No darkening or crumbling signs of age scarred the stone walls, and what few headstones there were appeared to be young and fresh: none had been smoothed by the passage of time. Several hundred metres away to their left stood the large, stone-built manor house which they had seen demolished in another age.

"What was that all about?" grunted Phillip as he stood up painfully, dusting himself down. Then: "What the...!"

Nadia spun to look at him.

He was dancing around in a most undignified manner, flicking at his leg. "Get off!"

She saw the spider taking evasive action, running up his flight suit towards his waist, and heard his breathing swiftly become shallow and laboured.

"Come here, keep still," she shouted, hurrying towards him. Despite his mounting panic he managed to bat the spider off and Nadia watched it scuttle away.

Phillip doubled over, resting his hands on his knees.

"Okay, okay. It's gone," she said, gripping his shoulder.

"Sorry," he panted. "You know what I'm like with spiders."

Realising his embarrassment at the phobia, Nadia quickly took her time placement recorder from its pouch, strapped securely to her waist, and switched it on, eager to bring him back to normality.

A slight frown creased her brow as its screen remained blank.

"What's happened to this?" she said, turning it over to look at its power level indicator. "Full power, but it won't come on."

A tiny red light glowed in the top right-hand corner, indicating that although the device was functioning properly it was not online with the timepod's computer system.

"I've no link with the pod," she said, fingering a sequence into the miniature keyboard. After a few seconds she shook her head. "Nothing. I can't get a thing from the main computer system. I can't even access it."

Phillip peered behind them, trying to see through the small thicket of young trees, with a worried look on his face. "We know the link works up to a thousand kilometres," he muttered, "*in the same time.*"

"What do you mean?"

He pointed in the direction they had come from. "The pod's gone, look."

She whirled around, her gaze following his outstretched finger.

"Or rather, *we've* gone," said Phillip, slowly. "The pod is probably still in the twentieth century. This looks more like where we first landed. Did you say it was the seventeenth century?"

Silently she nodded, trying to take in the horrendous consequences facing them if he were right—they were totally cut off from the timepod with no way of returning to it.

Suddenly she started running frantically towards where the ship should be. "It's got to be here somewhere," she screamed.

"Nadia!" Phillip gave chase, swiftly catching up with her. He grabbed her arm, spinning her to face him. Her eyes were wild and staring.

"Don't you understand, Phillip?" she cried. "If the pod didn't come with us we're stranded here. There's no way we can get home."

Her words descended into a fit of uncontrollable sobs, as she wildly looked around, straining to catch a glimpse of sunlight reflecting off the metal of their pod.

"It's got to be here." Her fingers jabbed at key after key, but elicited no response from the dormant device.

"Useless thing." She drew her arm back, ready to hurl the recorder into the bushes, but Phillip gripped her wrist.

"No, no," he said, gently prising her fingers from their precious piece of equipment. "This is our only chance of ever finding the pod again."

In their panic, they failed to notice a slight stirring in the bushes around twenty-five metres to their left. Two figures who had witnessed the travellers' apparently miraculous arrival, crept away towards the manor house, keeping close to the undergrowth. Once they were safely out of earshot and sight of the two strangers who were clad in silver-grey suits and boots, the man turned to his companion, a woman aged about twenty-one or so, wearing a slightly frayed and faded full-length brocade dress. His black, double-breasted jacket with its high lapels had also seen better days, as had the shiny breeches tucked into scuffed leather riding boots.

"They can say what they like, but there was no mistaking that." His voice was somewhat coarse, the words sounding breathless, through excitement rather than exertion. "I saw it with my own eyes, they were spirited here by a magic spell. The Reverend Crosskerry will have to believe me this time."

The girl remained silent while they walked past the side of the house and turned the corner, entering an L-shaped cobbled yard, bordered on two sides by the manor itself, and on two sides by a row of stables.

His eyes continued to shine with the same fervour and excitement, but Miranda Fengriffen wasn't so sure. "I don't know," she said, hesitantly, the softened vowels betraying her West Country origins. "They might have come through the trees and we just didn't see them."

"Well, I do know," replied Roger Partridge. "You do too, if the truth be told. You saw them suddenly appear."

Miranda wanted to believe, truly she did. But did these things really happen in the seventeenth century? Surely real witches had been hounded out of England years ago? The remaining covens weren't *real* witches, were they?

"And what about their strange dress?" continued Roger, Lord Berkeley's stable hand. "When did you see anyone wearing silver clothes like that?"

"I suppose you're right," Miranda admitted a little grudgingly. Four years ago, at the age of seventeen, she had arrived homeless and penniless in the swiftly-developing city of London, straddling the River Thames. The eldest of nine children, she had decided to leave the struggling family hovel on the bleak, barren north coast of Cornwall and head east, looking for a new settlement in which to make her fortune. She met Roger in an unsavoury tavern on the edge of town, and he took her back to Cranford Park, where the Earl of Berkeley employed her as a housemaid.

She felt grateful to Roger. After all, if it hadn't been for his kindness in befriending her she would never have this comfortable position now. But he wanted more than gratitude, and he took her for a walk into the sprouting woodland every other Wednesday afternoon when they had time off from their duties at the manor. She was a simple country girl, unused to the ways of the town—in particular to the ways of Roger Partridge.

His obsession with witches was something which disturbed her greatly, even though she fully understood his reasons: it was nearly three years since she had comforted him after the death of his parents.

A week after the Reverend Crosskerry had buried both his parents and his elder brother, Roger arranged a meeting with self-styled witch-finder Zephaniah Phips at a hostelry on the Bath Road. "I'm glad you've sought me out," Phips told him. "Are you a good Christian man, Mr. Partridge?"

"I like to think so, Mr. Phips. Of course, my duties at Cranford Park prevent me from going to church as often as I'd like. But the Reverend Crosskerry fully understands that."

"How well do you know your Bible, young man?"

"Ah, there you've got me." Roger coughed gently to hide his embarrassment. "I'm afraid I can't read," he half-whispered.

"The Bible tells you to turn the other cheek when you've been wronged."

The two tankards of ale leapt into the air, so powerfully did Roger's fist smash down on to the sturdy wooden table. "They're dead," he hissed. "My parents are dead. Killed by these filthy scum, and you say to turn the other cheek. Well, I won't do it, I tell you, I won't do it. If you won't help me I'll find someone who will."

He started to get up, but Phips put a restraining hand on his wrist. "Sit down, Mr. Partridge. Exodus chapter 22 verse 18."

"I told you I've never read the Bible." This time there was no discomfort, just raw anger.

"Thou shalt not suffer a witch to live," quoted Phips.

"So you'll help me?"

"If there's a genuine case here I'll pursue it and destroy the witches, yes. But, if all you seek is revenge for a crime, then this is not a job I will undertake. I must be totally convinced that the perpetrators of this abominable crime are Satan's followers. Tell me what you know."

All that Roger knew, he had been told by his brother Henry on his deathbed. "My parents and my elder brother had gone to Runnymede to celebrate the anniversary of the signing of the Magna Carta. It's a tradition the Partridge family have carried on ever since the sealing and issuing of the charter in 1215. In those far-off times my ancestors benefited greatly from the charter, and it's been passed down in my family from father to son through the generations that father, mother and firstborn son go to Runnymede on June fifteenth every year to celebrate the events which made our family great.

"Great!" he snorted. "We may have been once, but look at us now. I'm just a stable hand at Cranford Park."

"What happened to your parents and brother?" prompted Phips, not wanting to get embroiled in Partridge family history.

"Henry told me just before he died that they were settled at the inn were they were to sleep that night, having had a good quantity of venison and ale, when they decided to go for a walk. It was a moonlit night, and they thought a stroll by the river would be ideal. Unfortunately, on the way back they passed a churchyard where a witches' coven had also decided to make use of the moonlight. These foul beasts from hell were dancing naked around the gravestones. My mother gasped loud enough for the witches to hear.

"Before they knew it, they were being dragged into the churchyard and viciously beaten with stones. My brother was knocked unconscious and no doubt left for dead, as were my parents. They *were* dead when they were found by a parishioner the next day. My brother, however, lived for another five hours before he, too, died of his injuries. But not before he told me what had happened."

Zephaniah Phips was as good as his word. He discovered a witches' coven operating out of Runnymede. He left nothing to chance. Roger was all for rushing in at their next gathering and letting fly with a pair of pistols. But Phips calmed him down on the understanding that not one of the witches would escape.

And they didn't. Phips and his team infiltrated the coven and picked them off one by one.

However, Roger still refused to let the matter rest, imagining witchcraft in every corner, and the tainted touch of a coven on every person he met.

But Miranda had to confess that he might have something this time. Yes, she had seen the strangers appear out of thin air, there was no doubt about it. One moment she was giving Roger his fortnightly roll in the bracken, when suddenly the warm summer afternoon had been disturbed by an unnatural breeze, and there they were, the girl first, tumbling from nowhere, followed seconds later by the man.

Roger was right about the clothes, too. She had never seen anything like them before. The strangers wore identical silver-grey, all-in-one costumes, with the breeches tucked into four-inch boots—hardly the garb of the average visitor to Cranford Park. And tumbling out of the air was hardly the most conventional arrival.

Roger leaned back against the stable wall, recovering his breath. "You go and get the Reverend Crosskerry," he said. "I'll see where they go. We mustn't let them get away."

Miranda kissed him gently on the cheek. "Please be careful," she whispered.

Meanwhile, Phillip and Nadia were trying to take stock of exactly how much trouble they were in. A search of the immediate arrival site proved without doubt that the timepod was nowhere to be seen.

"It must have been the same disturbance that caught the pod in the first place," said Phillip. "It's dragged us three hundred years away."

Nadia was disconsolately keying sequences into the time placement recorder in another bid to access the pod's computer. She turned a miserable face towards him. "No joy with this. We're completely isolated."

Phillip sighed long and hard. "The only way we're going to get back is if another time disturbance picks us up again. And even then, the chances of it dropping us at the same date as the pod are—"

"—almost impossible," she finished for him. "I know. I think we've got to face it, Phillip, we're stuck here forever. Our ride home is parked three centuries in the future."

"What do you know about this era?"

"Not a thing. My history only goes back to the nineteenth century."

"Well, I think we'd better start trying to find out about it, if we've got to spend the rest of our lives here."

Nadia shivered and looked around. The prospect of living where fate had brought them was not a prospect she relished. "At least it's green," she conceded. "Not a concrete jungle like New London."

"Yes," mused Phillip. "Strange to think that TRAEP's headquarters are only about three or four miles in that direction."

"And only a few moments ago we were standing right here looking over towards Heathrow Airport."

"Now look at it. They haven't even discovered electricity yet."

Nadia turned away quickly, but not before Phillip caught a glimpse of a tear. "We're not going to survive here, are we?" she said, keeping her back to him. Training for this mission had covered many things, including learning how to use language from many eras of history. What it neglected to do, however, was prepare them for getting stranded in a remote time with no prospect of finding a way home.

"I must admit I'm not looking forward to living without the comforts we've become used to at home, but we haven't got much choice, have we?" He pointed towards the manor. "Maybe we can lodge there." he smiled. "I'll get a job as a butler and you can be the housekeeper. At least we'd have a comfortable roof over our heads."

Despite her fears, Nadia managed a hint of a smile. "Even if it is dark and cold."

"We'll survive alright," Phillip told her, trying to think of ways to keep her mind occupied and away from what he knew was a hopeless situation. "Think of the opportunities we've got—opportunities that no-one else in history has ever had. We can explore the world as it was in another era. We really will be pioneers."

Phillip's rumbling stomach turned his thoughts to their immediate problems, those of shelter and food. On the one hand it was several hours since they had eaten their last meal—on the other hand, it was about nine hundred years. And while it was a pleasantly warm day—they judged it to be the middle of summer—the nights were still likely to be chilly.

"Your idea about lodging at the manor wasn't so bad," said Nadia. "Why don't we see if they'll give us a meal and bed for the night in exchange for some work?"

"And what sort of work do you envisage us doing? I was joking, you know, when I said I could be the butler."

"Anything—cleaning, chopping wood. There'll always be something to do in a house that size, especially in this era with none of the modern conveniences that make life easier. There must be servants who could find us work. I'm sure they'll give us some food and let us sleep there, even if it is only on the floor. It'll be better than camping out here in the bracken."

"Now, there I agree with you," he said, thinking wistfully of the two small cots built into the wall of the timepod's cramped living quarters. *We never even got to sleep in them.* He remembered how derisive he and Nadia had been about them. "It's a good job I'm not claustrophobic," Nadia had said when they were being shown the pod for the first time. She had climbed into one to try it for size.

"That's Phillip's," their commander had told her. "Yours is the other one. They've been designed individually for you. You've each got ten centimetres to spare!"

Now, stranded centuries from home, he felt that a stone floor and blanket in the servants' quarters of a manor house heated by burning wood and lit by tallow candles, would be a desirable luxury. Compared to Nadia's alternative picture, painted so vividly and starkly, of sleeping under the stars in the bracken, he wondered if even a night in a stable might not also be considered luxurious.

"Come on, then," he said. "Let's go and see if we can persuade the good people of this house to put us up for the night."

Together they made their way towards the sweep of steps which rose to the massive oak front door.

"Shouldn't we find the servants' quarters at the back?" asked Nadia.

"Not a bit of it," replied Phillip briskly. "If we *have* to work for our board and lodgings, then so be it. But let's try the lost, weary traveller routine first, and see if the master of the house will invite us to dinner as his guests."

He tugged the bell-pull which dangled alongside the door, and they heard it echoing its insistent summons in the depth of the house. Several moments passed and Phillip was reaching out to give it another tug when the door swung silently aside.

Almost dwarfed by the huge archway which opened into the gloomy interior, stood a sombre-faced, elderly man, dressed from head to toe in black—forming rather an odd contrast to the lustre of the visitors' silver-grey attire. What little hair adorned his mottled head was white and wispy, curling somewhat untidily over his high collar. His back was slightly bent and his legs more than slightly bowed, clearly reflecting human frailty in its battle against the ravages of time.

"Yes?" His one word carried more strength and authority than either Nadia or Phillip had expected from the second or two they'd had to weigh him up.

"Good day, sir," began Phillip. "My companion and I are travellers on a long journey and have become separated from the rest of our party. We were hoping you may be able to give us shelter for the night, and perhaps a slice or two of bread and cheese for supper."

The old man's dim, rheumy eyes looked them up and down, and the hint of a raised eyebrow gave an indication of his surprise. "Travellers...?"

"Yes, sir," said Nadia. "My friend and I belong to a group of travelling players. We stopped at a tavern last night to perform our little show, and thanks to the inn-keeper's generous hospitality we fell asleep with our stomachs full of good meat and good ale. When we awoke this morning our fellow players had deserted us—"

"Thinking it a wonderful joke, no doubt," interrupted Phillip, looking at her sharply, wondering what on Earth she was talking about and hoping her convincing patter would not lead them into trouble.

Nadia cast him a cursory glance. "As my friend here surmises, a wonderful jest, no doubt, especially as they took our horses and luggage, leaving us with just the vestments you see us in."

Again Phillip looked at her, wondering whether he or the old man guarding their way was the more bemused. *I hope to goodness this is the sort of language he understands...vestments and jests, indeed.*

"Well, my master's something of a playgoer..." began the old man.

Nadia shot a swift look of triumph at Phillip.

"...but he's more for those plays by that fellow that died a few years back...what's his name, now, Shakespole, or something?"

"Shakespeare?" volunteered Nadia. "William Shakespeare?"

"Shakespeare...? Aye, I do reckon that's his name. My master's more for Shakespeare's plays than the sort of raucous thing you'd be performing, all dressed up like that." Once more his rheumy eyes scanned them up and down.

"No, no, no," insisted Nadia. "We are Shakespearean actors."

The old man's eyes widened in surprise. "You're allowed on the stage? Never."

"Oh no…not at all," countered Nadia quickly, realising her mistake. *Damn,* she thought, *it must be some time away before Margaret Hughes becomes the first woman to legally appear on stage in England.* For a fleeting moment she felt it truly strange that Shakespeare's great romantic tragedies could have become so popular with all the parts being played by men.

"I just help design the scenery and make the costumes."

For the third time in as many moments Phillip looked at his companion in amazement as she ploughed on, easily covering her error.

"Your master has excellent taste. Perhaps he may like to see our little show."

"If we can catch up with our troupe, of course," said Phillip.

"Where are you heading?" asked the butler.

That's got you, thought Phillip, smugly. He folded his arms in amusement and smiled at Nadia, wondering how she would extract herself from that one.

"Southwark," she said instantly. "We've got a show at the theatre there tomorrow."

"You'd best be coming in, then," said the old man, standing aside.

"I thought your history finished at the nineteenth century," Phillip hissed close in Nadia's ear as they followed him through the great hall.

"It does," she whispered back. "But my knowledge of Old English literature doesn't. And I specialised in the life and works of Shakespeare. I can virtually recite you all his plays."

"Some other time, perhaps. But seriously, Nadia, well done for getting us in here."

"If you'd wait in the library," said the butler, pushing open a set of double doors and indicating for them to go through. "I'll inform His Lordship you're here."

"Thank you, er…I'm sorry, we didn't catch your name?"

"Jacobs, my lady." He turned to leave.

"Well, thank you, Jacobs. There is just one more thing. Who is our noble host?"

"The Earl of Berkeley, ma'am." With that, Jacobs exited, closing the doors quietly behind him.

"Well, aren't you the one?" said Phillip, in grudging admiration.

"Surprised?"

"Not half. I didn't know you'd majored on Shakespeare in Old English literature."

"I certainly never thought it would come in so handy," she said, looking round at the opulent splendour of the book-lined walls. A gentle breeze wafted in through the slightly raised casement window.

"At least we know we're right about the time period," she said. "Jacobs told us Shakespeare died a few years ago—he died in 1616, so we're definitely somewhere in the early to middle part of the seventeenth century."

Phillip grinned at her. "I feel happier now I know how we're going to survive here."

"Pardon?"

"Well, I'll be acting, and you'll be designing my costumes…" He looked at their conspicuous clothes. "Oh, and just in case His Lordship asks, who am I meant to be playing?"

"You could always be Ariel, I suppose."

"Ariel?"

"The spirit, or fairy, from *The Tempest*. Typecasting, I'd say."

"Thanks a bunch."

"You're welcome," she grinned. "I suppose we ought to get our story straight."

"Yes, no more surprises, please."

"You're a fairy, okay?"

"Spirit."

"Spirit it is, then."

Outside the window Roger Partridge sank to the ground, sitting on the grass and leaning back against the wall, having heard the last part of their conversation. "So," he said to himself, softly. "Out of your own mouths, you're spirits, are you?"

He strained to hear a little more of what the two silver-clad strangers had to say. The silver-clad strangers he had seen literally fall out of thin air. The words floated over to him, first those of the man. "We've got to be very careful not to give ourselves away. We'll have to get rid of our watches…and goodness knows what these primitive people would make of your time placement recorder."

Then he heard the female speak: "But they're the only link we've got with our world."

Roger's eyes gleamed. "Our world." *Another admission from your own mouths.* He smiled as he twisted his head to peer up at the open window. *I've got you now, my friends. You're going straight back to your world. Burning you at the stake will send you on your way very nicely.*

* * *

"Welcome to Cranford Park." The deep voice belonging to the tall, aristocratic figure who threw open the library doors and strode inside, was mellow, yet authoritative at the same time, and very much in keeping with its owner's appearance. No wool for this man's clothes; a velvet smoking jacket covered what Phillip saw was a silk shirt as the newcomer moved towards them.

"I'm the Earl of Berkeley. Jacobs has been telling me what's happened to you. Most unfortunate."

"It's certainly that, my lord," said Nadia. "My name is Nadia, and this is my colleague, Phillip. We open at the Globe Theatre in Southwark tomorrow. And although Phillip has an understudy ready to take his part, the show won't be as good without its star."

"Fear not," smiled the earl. "You'll stay the night here as my honoured guests, and tomorrow we'll take my carriage to Southwark and find your troupe of players."

"That's very kind of you, my lord," began Nadia. "But there's really no need for you to go to all that trouble. We'll be perfectly happy with a good meal and a good night's sleep. Then we'll leave you in peace first thing in the morning. I'm sure we'll be able to find our own way to the Globe and catch up with our colleagues in time for the show."

"Nonsense, I wouldn't hear of it. You'd never get to Maiden Lane in time, on foot. You can repay my hospitality by taking me on a tour backstage when we get there. And you can give me the best seat in the house, too." There was a firm note of finality in the earl's voice, indicating that he was used to his every whim being obeyed without question.

"Well, if you put it like that, Your Lordship, how can we possibly refuse?"

The earl smiled at Phillip. "How, indeed, sir? That's settled then. We'll leave straight after breakfast. Now then, if you're giving me a tour of your domain tomorrow, I'd better give you a tour of mine, hadn't I? Come, I'll show you the house and grounds."

He ushered them through the doors back into the passage leading to the Great Hall. "I want to know all about your fascinating life on the road. But don't tell me which play you're currently putting on. Let it be a surprise for me tomorrow."

It'll be that, all right, thought Phillip. *Very definitely a surprise.*

"Tell me," said the earl. "What does your troupe of players call itself?"

* * *

When his nostrils flared in anger, as they were now, the Reverend William Crosskerry's red bulbous nose took on almost gigantic proportions. Its appearance was made even more grotesque by a somewhat shiny hue and the criss-crossing network of veins which spread to the rest of his face. It all bore testimony to more than a medicinal daily dose of fine French cognac. "So Partridge sends a woman to do his dirty work now, does he?" he huffed. "Go back to him, young lady, and tell him not to waste my time with any more stories of witches."

"If you please, sir…" Miranda half-curtsied, but the clergyman was already turning to walk back inside the rectory. Plucking up all her courage she gripped his shoulder. "I saw them, too. I think he could be right this time."

The Reverend Crosskerry was always impressed by Miranda's down-to-earth manner, and he knew that she played an important role in bringing Roger Partridge to his senses after that awful business with his parents. Also, she had helped the vicar to talk sense into him on the numerous occasions he made wild accusations about witchcraft in their small community. So, if she said Partridge may be right, perhaps he ought to listen, at least.

"Very well, my child." A comforting arm went around her shoulders, but his hand reached down unnecessarily towards her left breast. "Come inside and tell me what you saw."

He listened, half in amazement and half in disbelief, as Miranda sat in his study telling of strangers clad in peculiar silver-grey garments literally tumbling out of thin air.

"One moment there was nothing, then suddenly they were right there. We saw them quite clearly from the bushes."

At any other time the Reverend Crosskerry would have wanted to know what she and Partridge had been doing in the bushes. His hand squeezed her breast. But from what she was saying, there were more important matters at the moment. "Where are they right now?"

"Roger was keeping watch while I came for you, sir. I beg of you, please come back with me."

* * *

From his vantage point behind the small summerhouse on top of a hillock, Roger saw Miranda and the vicar hurrying along the path from the woods, in which stood the rectory. A turn of his head, and he caught a glimpse of the Earl of Berkeley with the two strangers on the far side of the house, heading towards the ornamental pool.

He beckoned to Miranda, who returned his wave. In a few moments she dropped down beside him. He was pleased to see the vicar had brought a Bible.

"What's all this about, Roger?" said Crosskerry, making a big show of wiping the sweat from his forehead. "It's a warm evening to be undertaking such excursions."

"Has Miranda told you about the witches?"

The vicar nodded. "She said two strangers appeared out of nowhere."

"I heard them talking," added Roger, somewhat excitedly. "They spoke of *their world* and confessed they were spirits."

"Where are they now?"

"They're with His Lordship. He's showing them round the estate."

"Then I think we'll confront them on their return," said Crosskerry. "Perhaps we should wait in the house where you can fortify my depleted strength with a drop of His Lordship's excellent cognac."

* * *

"Oh, is he now?" said the Earl of Berkeley when Jacobs told him the vicar was in the study. "Would you kindly inform him I have guests, and now is not a convenient time for me? I'll see him tomorrow morning, and then...ah, no, I won't. I'll be in Southwark at the Globe Theatre in the morning." He smiled at Nadia and Phillip. "Tell him to call for afternoon tea the day after tomorrow."

Jacobs coughed uncomfortably. "He was quite insistent, sir, and he did say he needed to talk to you about...er...your guests, sir."

Phillip and Nadia traded a nervous glance.

"I apologise for this," said Lord Berkeley. "But if I don't talk to the wretched fellow he'll probably hang around for days, making a nuisance of himself. I'd better go and see what he wants. Please excuse me. I won't be long."

He turned back to Jacobs. "Get Chambers to show our guests to their rooms."

"Very good, sir."

Lord Berkeley strode from the room while Jacobs shuffled slowly to the door, pausing when he got there. "Chambers is the housekeeper, sir. She'll be with you in a moment."

Nadia gave the servant her most charming smile. "No hurry, Jacobs, thank you."

"I don't like the sound of this," said Phillip, after Jacobs had closed the door behind him. "What can a vicar want with us?"

"He's probably heard there's a fairy in town and wants to book you for the church show."

"Funny."

* * *

"Witches!"

"I'm afraid it looks that way, Your Lordship. Young Miranda Fengriffen's backing his claims this time."

"Nonsense. It's just Partridge up to his old tricks again. If he doesn't stop making these wild accusations I'll have to let him go and find myself a new stable hand. And I'd have expected better from you, Vicar."

"All I ask, sir, is that I be allowed to question them."

"No. And that's the end of it, Crosskerry. They're my guests and I won't let you pester them."

"But what about their strange clothes and the way they suddenly appeared from nowhere?"

"They're from an acting troupe. They were left stranded at an inn. Their clothes are, at this very moment, on their way to Maiden Lane in Southwark. Now, good day to you, Reverend. Jacobs will show you out."

* * *

Phillip had to admit that Nadia looked stunning as she made her way down the staircase to where he and the earl sat in the Great Hall, each with a glass of powerful red wine. Phillip also had to admit that the wine was surprisingly smooth. He had been expecting something much rougher, given the era they were now stranded in.

The delicately embroidered, flowing black gown with white collar which Nadia now wore was a stark contrast to her normal wardrobe, but the earl had insisted she borrow something of his late wife's, for dinner.

"My cook is French, so you'll notice a distinct foreign influence over the fare we're about to eat," said the earl after they moved into the dining room. "Look at this." He indicated the feast spread out before them. "She has regaled us with some excellent coulis, roux, ragouts, and fricassé tonight. Oh, and her anchovies and capers are exquisite."

Phillip and Nadia exchanged a quick glance. Maybe they were going to be happy in this century after all.

The earl caught the glance, and perhaps misinterpreted it. "Sorry. I do go on a bit, don't I? It's since my wife died. Whenever I have visitors I make up for the lack of civilised, intelligent company by —"

"Please don't apologise, my lord. It's not often on our travels that we enjoy intelligent, civilised company either. Please go on."

"Very well, young man…as long as I'm not boring you. I suspect that following the king's marriage to Henrietta Maria two years ago the political unison between our two countries will extend more and more into sharing foods too. Queen Consort Henrietta is renowned for her love of food and I'm sure she's making the culinary delights of her native France a regular occurrence on the tables at court."

The earl cast a swift look at his guests. "Not that I'm completely sure of our new monarch, though. I don't think he's cut from the same cloth as his father. And his marriage is not popular amongst his regular subjects, of course, but they don't share our excellent taste in French food, do they."

"The king—Charles the First," said Nadia. "Yes, he was…is…."

"The first!" laughed the Earl. "He's certainly that. I don't know of any other. Even before James claimed the monarchy for the House of Stuart."

Nadia turned towards Phillip to hide the redness which rushed up her face. "No," she stumbled. "I mean he's the first king to be called Charles."

Phillip came to her rescue: "We hear such different tales about him on our travels," he said. "Some people like him, others don't."

"It's a little early in his reign for the commoners to see his value," said the earl. "I suppose time will tell what he's really like." He motioned toward the door, where Jacobs and Miranda Fengriffen were standing. "I think we're ready to eat."

Jacobs moved forward with a half smile. "Certainly my lord."

But Phillip noticed Miranda stayed stony-faced throughout. *There's something about that girl I don't trust*, he thought. And he was particularly concerned when the earl mentioned the reason for Croskerry's visit, when they were halfway through dinner.

Nadia had brought it up: "Forgive me for asking, my lord, but are you able to tell us why the vicar wanted to talk to you about us? We don't even know him."

"Don't you worry about that old fool. Apparently when he saw you coming towards the village he was somewhat startled by your unconventional appearance."

Miranda caught Phillip's troubled glance at Nadia, but of course had no way of knowing the disturbing thought which passed through his mind: *How could the vicar have seen us approaching the village? We were no more than a few hundred metres from the house when we arrived in this time. He couldn't have seen us.*

* * *

In daylight Miranda knew exactly which step creaked, but with only candlelight to guide her down the servants' staircase she wasn't so sure. Tentatively she placed her slippered feet on each step, slowly increasing the pressure before moving on to the next one. Not that she need worry—at three o'clock in the morning the rest of the house was sound asleep. Holding the candle in front of her she made her way through the scullery to the door leading out on to the cobbled yard.

A candle flickered in the window of Roger's room above the stables. Slowly she moved her own small flame from left to right and back again—their prearranged signal.

A moment later, Roger stood beside her. "Well done," he hissed.

"Do you really need me?" she whispered. "I'd rather not be part of this."

"Of course I need you. I can't drag them through the passage by myself. You saw the size of the male witch. He's six feet tall if he's an inch. And we'll have to work fast."

Miranda swallowed nervously. Yes, she had seen Phillip's troubled glance at Nadia when the earl mentioned the vicar's visit. *That look said it all.*

Now, here she was in the early hours of the morning, opening the hidden panel in the library, giving Roger access to the maze of secret passages and tunnels which riddled the house. Even with candles to light their way, the journey through the bowels of the manor was dark and slow. But eventually they reached the panel which Miranda said opened into the male witch's bedchamber.

The back of the fireplace swung aside with a faint squeak. Stealthily, Roger crouched through the secret doorway and peered towards the sleeping form of Phillip Oatridge in the lavish four-poster bed. He reached back inside the passage and took a heavy stick from Miranda. Then he made his way to the bed and brought the stick crashing down with sickening force on the side of Phillip's head. With a groan, Phillip's deep, comfortable sleep turned into unconsciousness.

Silently Miranda joined Roger, and together they dragged the comatose form into the secret passage, before she pushed a lever set in the wall to close the panel.

A few moments later the scene was re-enacted in Nadia's room. Miranda held both candles, which were not doing terribly well in combating the piercing darkness of the hidden passage. Roger rolled both unconscious prisoners onto their stomachs and securely bound their hands behind their back, before tying their ankles together. Then began the arduous task of carrying them, one at a time, back through the passage and out to the courtyard where they had left a small handcart.

The unconscious travellers were dumped into the cart and, taking a handle each, Roger and Miranda hauled it away from the manor and out to the woods.

The moonlight washed over them, illuminating their way, making it simpler for Roger to find the approximate spot where he had seen the witches appear. Somewhere nearby an owl hooted. Its mate responded with a similar call.

"Burning them at the place where they entered our world will make it easier to send them back through the doorway to hell," he had explained to Miranda earlier, while they piled kindling around the base of two sturdy trees, forming rings almost a metre deep.

"I wish you'd wait for the Reverend Crosskerry," she told him. "You know he's ridden to London to fetch the witch hunter. We should give them a proper trial."

"By the time they get back here in the morning it'll all be over," Roger had said, a malicious gleam lighting his eyes. "The evidence of my own ears and eyes is all the proof I need."

And now it *would* soon be all over. Using two more pieces of stout rope he bound Phillip and Nadia's unconscious forms to the two trees before stepping back in triumph.

"Again, vengeance for my parents," he cried. "Two less accursed followers of Satan. What I do now, I do in the name of the Almighty Father, who tells us in his Holy Bible: 'Thou shalt not suffer a witch to live.'"

Reaching into his jacket pocket he brought out a small tinder box and lit the wick, holding the tiny flame to the dry kindling spread out at Nadia's feet. With a sudden crackle the flame leapt to the wood, darting from piece to piece.

"May your souls rot in hell!" Roger thundered as he held the tinder box to the wood surrounding Phillip. Within seconds the fire was burning fiercely around both trees.

Nadia's first befuddled thought was that her head ached abominably. And the second was that she couldn't raise her hands to rub her eyes. She looked in terror at the flames which were now licking at her ankles, and suddenly she was wide awake, her arms straining in futile efforts to break free of the bonds holding her securely to the tree.

"Phillip!" she screamed at the top of her voice. "Help, Phillip!"

The crackling grew in intensity as fingers of flickering fire consumed the kindling on an unbarred path leading to the centre of the rings. The wood popped and snapped, and tiny flecks of ash swirled upwards in grey smoke.

Phillip's first waking thought was that he was still in the grip of his nightmare, where he was trapped by his safety harness in the pilot's seat aboard the timepod. The vessel had crashed, and all around him the flames were rising ever higher into the air. Somewhere alongside him, presumably trapped in her seat, too, he could hear Nadia's frantic yelling. Then he awoke, but the screams continued. So did the flames. So did the crackling. So did the heat. So did the nightmare. He snapped his head upright.

"What the...?" Wildly his eyes took in the scene, illuminated almost to daylight by the baleful eye of the full moon staring down amidst the billions of stars.

"Help us," he implored of the man and woman standing beyond the ring of fire completely surrounding the two trees.

But the only response came from the man, who was now grinning insanely, and Phillip saw the flames reflecting from his eyes in a mad gleam. "'Thou shalt not suffer a witch to live!'" he yelled. "Burn, witches! Burn, witches, burn!"

The woman took up the chant in unison, their joint voices rising to an almost unbearable crescendo above the fire's relentless spitting.

The first fingers of flame began to caress Nadia's bare leg, reaching for the hem of the nightgown borrowed from one of the maids. Her screams echoed madly around the copse while she frantically looked for a way out.

But none was to be had.

Her chafed wrists began to bleed as she pulled with all her might against the ropes, but she was held as securely as before. Twisting her legs, she attempted to snap the ropes holding her ankles, but only succeeded in driving splinters of wood into her bare feet.

It was likely that realisation dawned on Phillip and Nadia at the same instant—the tips of the highest flames were now level with their elbows, inching towards their writhing bodies, while some of the nearer, lower ones were already beginning to scorch their flesh; the intense heat becoming unbearable. Nothing could stop the fire from consuming their bodies within seconds.

As their screams echoed around the copse, travelling deeper through the trees, the two owls hooted in alarm and ascended from their branches, seeking a quieter, more peaceful haven.

CHAPTER 5

THE BRINK OF ETERNITY

CAITLIN WAS FLUNG LIKE A RAG DOLL around the floor of the shuttle. Ashday's Child noted grimly that a splash of blood followed her every move. Then, as she rolled onto her left side he saw the ragged gash on her temple.

Half a minute had now elapsed since the computer's level twenty warning, and because it was apparently being ignored, the alarm system cut in automatically. An urgent, insistent siren filled the cabin—not that Ashday's Child needed any more incentive; he had already unbuckled his lap belt and was reaching for the back of the pilot's seat.

"Critical level in one minute ten seconds," the computer told him, dispassionately. "Destruction of shuttle irreversible in one minute thirty seconds."

His fingers were just centimetres short of gripping the headrest when the shuttle bucked violently, sending him sprawling to the floor. For a second or two the shuttle's passage, riding the front of the temporal wave, grew smoother, enabling him to finally hook an arm around the pilot's seat. He fought his way to his knees, inching round to the front of the chair, holding on for grim death when an upsurge raised the vessel's nose into the air. Then, on the downstroke, the shuttle's own momentum carried him forward—but too far. The breath was knocked from his body as he crashed into the control console before flopping back onto the seat.

His hand was reaching for the lap belt to strap himself into the pilot's control chair when he heard the warning.

"Critical level approaching," said the computer. "Destruction of shuttle irreversible in fifty seconds." *No time for this,* he thought. *Got to get us out of here. Now.* His hand hovered just above the strap, then changed direction, aiming instead for the booster controls. *Must fire boosters, must get away from this wave.*

Without warning, the shuttle yawed severely, throwing Ashday's Child from the safety of his seat, his windmilling arms proving ineffective on two counts: failing to keep him upright, and failing to power the boosters.

Above the crescendo of the sirens he could hear the computer's impassive intonation: "Critical level surpassed. Irreversible destruction of shuttle in twenty seconds."

The shuttle was not built to protect its passengers from the incredible g-forces they were now experiencing. The temporal distortion swept it onwards through uncharted time at an ever increasing velocity. The flesh of Ashday's Child's face contorted in undulating folds as he made one last supreme effort to raise up and hurl himself forward. Half a metre more and he'd have made it. As it was, his fingers closed on empty air, and in response to another lurch from the errant craft, he rolled over, smashing the back of his head against the seat's metal strut.

Somewhere deep in his immense energy reserves he could hear the computer issue its final warning.

Then spinning stars. Blackness. Ashday's Child fell unconscious.

On and on the shuttle raced through unfathomable aeons, the g-forces generating almost intolerable pressure.

Suddenly those g-forces subsided and the shuttle's rocketing speed diminished. Everything not fastened down was flung forward, including the craft's two occupants. They were flattened against the rounded wall at the front, as the shuttle spun, veered and rocked.

"Manual controls overridden," announced the computer. "Automatic emergency circuits locked online."

Ashday's Child never knew how long he lay unconscious, sprawled across the top of the control console, almost smothering Caitlin. He felt he was in a darkened tunnel moving slowly towards the light and as the light came nearer his senses began to recover. Ignoring the stabbing pain in his head he eased himself to his feet and lifted

Caitlin into her seat. His eyes focused on the dead instruments which told him the computer had drained all the ship's power except for the emergency life support systems, meaning heat and light were now at an absolute minimum.

"Computer, what happened?" he asked, easing Caitlin's head around so he could look at her wound.

"Emergency circuits overrode all manual control to preserve shuttle by outrunning distortion waves. Power needed to escape from temporal distortion was ninety-eight percent of total shuttle capability. Remaining two percent is sustaining minimum life support."

His eyes scanned the panels in front of him, but all computer screens and digital readouts were blank.

"Computer, put present speed and date on to the instrument readout."

Instantly the dim glow of the lights faded even more as the computer transferred enough power to the console to bring the two relevant screens to life. His eyes widened as their incredible speed registered in his mind. "Why are we still going so fast?"

"All available power resource was put into braking forward acceleration and achieving enough reverse velocity to safely escape the wave."

"So the shuttle is now hurtling backwards in time, not forwards any more, and we don't have enough power to stop? Is that it?"

"Affirmative."

"When will we have recharged enough power to stop?"

"All regenerated power is constantly being transferred to braking system. Combined with natural inertia the shuttle will be able to carry out effective braking and come to a halt in three hours, nine minutes and forty-five seconds."

He looked at the date readout which simply showed *Insufficient data*. "Is there no way of stopping before then?"

"Negative."

"How far forward in time did the wave take us?"

"Unable to calculate. No co-ordinates were set before we commenced this journey. Therefore there is insufficient data to compute."

A moan from Caitlin took his attention and he cupped her chin in his hands. She opened her eyes with a grimace.

"Welcome back to the world," he said.

"Oh, my head." She touched the wound caused when the shuttle had thrown her against the wall. "Oowww." She pulled her hand away sharply, looking at the traces of blood on it. "I must have taken quite a crack. What happened?"

"I'll explain in a moment. In the meantime, let's see if I can find the medical kit amongst this mess."

Ashday's Child cleaned Caitlin's wound before expertly closing it with a laser suture. "There we go," he said, stepping back to admire his handiwork. A faint, six centimetre long red line ran beside her right eye, ending in a slight curl beneath it. "In a couple of days that'll be gone and you'll look as good as new." He switched off the pencil-like device and returned it to its slot amongst the other medical instruments.

Caitlin winced as she touched the scar. "A pity it doesn't take the pain away as easily."

"Go and rest while I clear up in here. There's nothing more we can do for several hours, anyway."

"Okay, thanks."

"No worries."

"Life's never dull around you, is it?"

"So they tell me. Go and get some rest – no falling asleep, though, yet; not after that bang on the head. I'll take us home. You deserve a break. You took me to Australia, then London, and you had to put up with me on the plane to and from Austria. You've been on the go a long time."

Caitlin touched the scar again. "Yeah, I will. My head's banging." She disappeared into her tiny cubicle, and Ashday's Child eased himself back into her seat.

The only evidence that the shuttle was even moving lay in a faint swaying sensation that came every so often when a little more of the newly-generated power brought on board from the essence of the Timeshaft itself, through the craft's external sensors, transferred to the braking system.

Ashday's Child did a quick mental calculation and worked out that if he switched minimum power to the video communication circuits for a five-minute conversation with Shuttle Management

Control at WorldSave headquarters, the end of their journey would only be delayed by a further fifteen minutes. He turned on the communicator and re-routed power through the computer's switching board. In a few moments he had sufficient build-up to directly access WorldSave's comms link, alerting the operators that they had an incoming message.

The multimedia system flickered into life and from somewhere across the centuries the face of a communications assistant flowed onto the screen.

"Receiving you, Ashday's Child. Where are you? We've lost all contact with you on the Timeshaft monitors."

"That's a very good question. The brink of eternity, I reckon. But I was hoping you'd be able to tell me for sure."

"Sorry, no can do. Apparently the TRAEP timepod damaged the shaft on its very first voyage, and you got caught up in it. That's all I know for sure." The comms assistant glanced to his left, and spoke to someone just out of view.

"Yes, it is. He's just made contact," he said to the unseen person beside him. He looked back into the lens.

"Dr. Gannaton would like to speak to you, sir."

"Okay, patch me through."

Instantly the picture switched to a brown-haired, brown-eyed man a good forty years younger than Ashday's Child: Dr. Bob Gannaton, chief executive of WorldSave.

"Thank goodness you're all right. We thought we'd lost you there."

"We're both a bit battered and bruised but we'll survive. Do you know what happened?"

"Yes. Problems with Phillip Oatridge and Nadia Reeder's inaugural flight for the Time Research and Exploration Project two hundred years ago. According to our technicians, who've been monitoring the situation very closely, there was apparently some difficulty with their pod's drive technology. It looks as if it might have been too primitive to tap into the Timeshaft dimension for a stable temporal flight. It seems to have gone wrong on two counts. First of all, its radiation emissions caused a series of temporal displacement waves to shoot through the shaft—the last time we registered your shuttle you were caught in the tip of one racing into the far future.

"Our equipment shows that the disturbance also knocked TRAEP's pod off course, but while they were attempting to land they tore a hole in the kinetic energy binding the shaft's matrix. The hole stretches from the seventeenth century to the end of the twentieth."

A sudden gleam shone in Ashday's Child's weasel eyes. *The seventeenth century! This could be it, this has to be it,* he thought. *My destiny approaches at last.* A half smile played on his lips, which he fought back before the chief executive could see it.

"There's more, though," continued Dr. Gannaton. "Oatridge and Reeder have been catapulted through that hole without their pod. They parked in the twentieth century and promptly fell into the energy swirl seeping through the rip. It's left them stranded about 350 years away from their vehicle."

He paused a moment. Then: "We need you to rescue them and take them back to their pod."

"No problem, but it'll have to wait awhile." Ashday's Child explained what had happened to his shuttle.

"Okay," said Dr. Gannaton. "I'll download the TRAEP vehicle's co-ordinates to your computer, along with the co-ordinates for where you'll find Nadia Reeder and Phillip Oatridge. As soon as you're back to full power I'd like you to pick them up and drop them off at their pod. By the time you get them there our engineers will have modified their drive system to prevent any more radiation emissions."

"What about the hole in the matrix?" asked Ashday's Child. "Will it still cause us problems when we reach that era?"

"Could do. Our team will be working on that as well, but they estimate it'll take at least a couple of days, real time, before they've stopped all the time fluctuations. Our main concern at the moment, though, is whether there'll be any more temporal displacement waves. We're not able to stop a recurrence of those until the rip's been sealed."

"Are there likely to be any more? I'd have thought they'd be dispersed by now. And if the pod's being modified there won't be any new ones, will there?"

"Our computer predictions are that at least three more are loose somewhere in the Timeshaft. We've only been able to account for three, but the energy released from the pod could create double that number. Communications are monitoring as far along the shaft in both directions as they can, and they'll alert you if they spot anything. Meanwhile, keep your on-board computer probes set to maximum. You'll need as much time as possible to take evasive action if there are any more about."

"Right, thanks for the warning."

"Leave your circuits open for a couple of minutes while I arrange for those co-ordinates to be downloaded to you. And good luck. See you soon."

Ashday's Child cut the video link, but ensured the computer was still online to receive the necessary data to rescue the stranded time travel pioneers.

Relaxing in the pilot's chair, he smiled, wondering if at long last his career could be coming to a close. If what Dr. Gannaton told him was true, about the hole in the Timeshaft stretching to the seventeenth century, was he about to find the one essential missing piece in his life? The spur that had kept him going all these years? Would he shortly be able to take the retirement he had yearned after for so long? *This must be it. I've been waiting for this for fifty years. All I've got to do now is —*

His thoughts were interrupted by a movement behind him. Caitlin stood in the open doorway leading from the living quarters.

"I thought you were getting some rest," he said.

"I heard you contact base and just wondered if they knew what had happened to us. It's all down to that first experimental voyage through time then?"

"It looks like it, yes."

"But you told me that WorldSave gave TRAEP the secret of time travel in the first place."

Ashday's Child nodded slowly. He could guess what was coming next.

"So why were they allowed to use a vehicle which would damage the shaft?" she wanted to know.

But for his conversation with Dr. Gannaton a few moments ago Ashday's Child would not have been able to hazard a guess. But now it all began to make sense. "Do you believe in destiny?" he asked.

Caitlin blinked. "Destiny…? I don't follow you."

"I think something's about to happen that's pre-ordained. Something that's already shaped the course of history. The Timeshaft may never have existed without it. WorldSave's work across the centuries during these last fifty years wouldn't have been possible, and the world itself would have been destroyed six hundred years before you were born."

"And we're going to this event, whatever it is that's going to happen, right now?" she asked, incredulously.

"I rather think we may be. But it's nothing terribly exciting. If it's what I think it is, all that'll happen is that we'll take a couple of extra passengers on board in the next few hours."

"Yes, I know that. I heard you talking to Dr. Gannaton."

"My dear girl," he said. "Very soon you'll understand. No, I'm not talking about those other time travellers. I believe that before we pick up our time-travelling pioneers we'll be meeting another young couple. And if I'm not very much mistaken they'll be most anxious that we bring them along for the ride."

Caitlin was bordering on exasperation. "What's going on?"

Her only answer was his enigmatic smile.

"Come on," she insisted. "You've got to tell me."

"Not yet. I may be wrong. But if I'm right…well, you'll know soon enough."

SECTION TWO

ASHDAY'S CHILD

CHAPTER 6

THIECON LORE

WITH EACH PASSING WEEK the ritual grew more poignant and he dreaded the prospect of walking across the plain to the towering stone pillars of the mighty henge.

And when the Holy Man and Star-Gazer extended their arms heavenward to praise the All-Seeing-All-Powerful-One for the coming of another seven dawns, he felt every eye was on him, knowing of his sin.

Yet how could they know? The secret lay buried deep in his own heart, shared only with Laoni. But he kept asking himself how long it would be before her body began to swell as the child within her grew, exposing their guilt to the village.

It was not the result of deliberate defiance, just one moment of rashness, but he knew the elders wouldn't see it that way. Laoni knew, too—the wild-eyed look of terror on his partner's face when she confessed would haunt him forever.

That was when his nightmare started.

* * *

The sun had been powerful all day and during the last couple of hours Jontil's thoughts turned with eager anticipation to a jug or two of the strong ale which Laoni was so good at brewing. When the beasts were taken care of for the day he began the short walk home through the sloping strip of woodland separating his three acres from the village.

As he passed the last sycamore the countryside opened up before him, rolling away to its distant rendezvous with the evening sky. He looked down upon the scores of huts scattered along the river bank; the thread of water trailing through the foot of the valley as far as the eye could see.

Laoni had promised him the tender white meat of a fatted young calf for his supper, and the twist of greyish-black smoke worming its way through the roof of his hut told him the food was already cooking over a charcoal fire. Many other huts gave off smoke, too—he would not be the only one feasting on good cooked meat that night.

He sensed something was wrong as soon as he flipped aside the lengths of hanging beads and stepped into the cool, darkened interior of his home.

"Laoni, why've you got the windows covered? There's still daylight outside."

Instead of answering, she continued to squat by the fire with her back to him, gently prodding the spit-roasting meat. Normally she would run to him, her bare feet slapping against the earthen floor, and throw herself into his arms.

"Laoni?" he called again, staring at the back of her knee-length light brown tunic and noticing her shoulders trembling slightly. There was also a tremor running through the sleek raven-black hair, as if she were rapidly nodding her head. Then he could see that her whole body was wracked with sobs.

As he hurried towards her she suddenly stood up and spun to face him. Red rings surrounded the dark brown eyes and her breath came in rough, uneven gasps. He clasped her to his chest, stroking her hair soothingly.

"Come on," he whispered. "What is it? What's wrong?"

She eased herself away from his grip and ran to the beading, peering out into the fading daylight. Then she turned back to him and led the way through the arch into the more comfortable living area of the hut. That, too, was in semi-darkness; she had draped a blanket over the window in there, as well.

He stood in silence, waiting for her to tell him what was troubling her.

"Oh, Jontil," she eventually managed to murmur between sobs. "Whatever's going to become of us?"

"What's wrong?" he repeated, smiling into her eyes to try and reassure her that whatever it was they would face it together.

She looked up at him with a haunted, fear-ridden face, and shook her head slowly. It was almost as if the words were fighting to come, but she was desperately trying to suppress them.

"I've been meaning to tell you..." she began, then stopped, turning to stare blankly at the wall.

An eternity seemed to pass before Jontil reluctantly accepted he would have to prompt her. He put his hand beneath her quivering chin and gently eased her towards him again.

"Tell me what, darling?"

"It just never seemed to be the right moment. I was always so frightened. I'm scared, Jontil, so scared."

His heart grieved to see her this upset. While his fingers softly caressed her long dark hair his frown deepened as he tried to imagine what could be troubling her so much.

"Tell me, Laoni," he said, gently. "Please tell me what it is. I can't help you unless I know."

She took a deep breath, holding it in her lungs for longer than was comfortable, causing a red flush to race up her cheeks. When she did eventually manage to speak the words cascaded out in a mad jumbled rush.

"Jontil, please don't be cross with me. I love you so much. I'd never do anything to hurt you or put you in danger. You know that, don't you? I'll go away or kill myself, then no-one'll ever know. Oh, what am I going to do? What...?"

"Hey, steady on. Come on, now, slow down and tell me what it is." There was something about the unusual blackness of her mood and the uncharacteristic hysteria which emitted a grim, foreboding aura. Jontil started to pull her face towards his chest, but she broke away, taking a couple of steps backwards.

Again a deep breath; then finally it was out: "Jontil, I'm going to have a baby — *we're* going to have a baby."

Something nagged at the back of his mind, but his thoughts were instantly filled with what he imagined to be the usual euphoria of a would-be father, and he started to laugh.

"A baby!" he cried. "But that's wonderful. Why all the tears? Why the worry? Didn't you think I'd be pleased? I'm so happy, it's wonderful news."

She clasped a hand over his mouth. "Shhh. Quiet!" Her voice was low, demanding, insistent.

But again Jontil laughed as he softly prised her fingers away from his face. "I don't understand what's worrying you." His mind whirled in a plethora of happy, wondrous thoughts. He was going to be a father.

Her soft, delicate features were stained by tiny rivulets of tears, and she shook her head urgently, her face a mixture of fear and frustration.

"Jontil, *think*. I'm just over a Quarter Year pregnant. The baby will be born in the forbidden Second Quarter of the New Year. We're going to have an Ashday's Child."

That simple phrase slammed into him with all the force of a wooden club. A few seconds of numbness rooted him to the spot, giving her a chance to wrap her arms around his shoulders and cling tightly to him.

He pushed her away as if she were suddenly as hot as fire. "Oh my God. The Second Quarter. An *Ashday's Child*. Are you sure?" His momentary happiness at the prospect of becoming a father evaporated in a horrifying split second.

Laoni took a couple of paces away from him, looking small and vulnerable, her head drooping.

"I'm sure," she said. "I've been sure for weeks. We'll bring disgrace to the village." Her voice was rising all the time, verging on the borders of hysteria. "It'll be…"

"Okay, okay." Jontil pulled her towards him again before the significance of what she had just said suddenly hit him. He spun her sideways, staring hard at her stomach, looking for signs of the child. There was nothing tangible apart from some recent stitching at the side of her tunic, suggesting she may have let it out a little.

"If you've known for weeks why didn't you tell me, give me time to work something out?" he demanded.

"Don't worry," she said, smiling through the tears, seeming to regain a little more composure now her secret was out. "If I'm careful it doesn't show yet."

Jontil stared at the ceiling, his mind running away with itself, his thoughts tumbling over each other.

"Why didn't you tell me before?" he asked again. "You must stay indoors and I'll say you're ill."

Suddenly he gripped her shoulders and shook her hard. "Don't you understand what this means? They'll execute us. What we've done is blasphemy, a sin against the All-Seeing-All-Powerful-One. We've sinned against God." Now it was his turn to edge towards hysteria.

He closed his eyes, remembering when the village had been awakened by the Destroyers of Evil thundering out of the night on horseback to descend on the home of their friends Brantis and Leila, whisking them away to the henge. The following day an expectant buzz had pervaded the air during their trek to the weekly thanksgiving. Brantis and Leila had been brought out and thrust before the massed gathering. The Star-Gazer was almost consumed with fury during his hellfire sermon about breaking the golden rule of their civilisation: conceiving a child which, if allowed to be born, would enter the world during the forbidden Second Quarter; an *Ashday's Child*.

Jontil shuddered as he recalled how his voice had raised against his friends; how it was filled with hate and righteousness when he joined the chanted demands that they be stoned to death in accordance with the ancient laws. The Holy Man commanded a degree of calm as he began the stoning ceremony by reminding the gathering of the sin Brantis and Leila had committed…

The Holy Man's arms were raised heavenward and his voice was strong as he began the ancient ceremony with the words that were only summoned for the cleansing ritual: "It all began long, long ago, in the days before the world died; in the days before the All-Seeing-All-Powerful-One rebuilt the world by His own magic. Before the Great Fire fanned by the Winds of Destruction blighted our land. Our realm was not as you see it today. The world was full of mechanised monsters, of great metal birds capable of taking Man in their hollow bellies from one land to another.

"Evil and wickedness controlled men's lives everywhere. There were many false star-gazers, each claiming to be able to read messages from the heavens; such as our own—the only true—Star-Gazer does today. Our true Star-Gazer succeeds because he draws his power from the All-Seeing-All-Powerful-One. Those charlatans of ancient time did not; their power was false and evil, in defiance of the Holy Orders of the day.

"Man became pitted against Man. Nation against nation. As Man's intelligence grew, his wisdom diminished, and his technology was used for evil, for destruction. Destruction of countries, destruction of continents. Immediately after the tribulation of those days the sun darkened, and the moon did not give its light. The stars fell from heaven and the powers of the heavens were shaken. After our civilisation eventually rose from the ashes, the All-Seeing-All-Powerful-One decreed that such carnage would never return to the earth. He blessed the family of the Star-Gazer with hereditary power to truly read the signs of the heavens, so Mankind would be warned through all eternity of that which was yet to come. That awesome and terrible power has spanned the generations to our Star-Gazer of today, who continues the tradition begun by His forefathers.

"His power, guided by the All-Seeing-All-Powerful-One, has shown the downfall of our former brother Brantis and our former sister Leila. By conceiving a child whose birth would fall within the forbidden Second Quarter—the deadly quarter when ash fell upon the earth from the Great Fire, fanned by the Winds of Destruction— they have sinned against us all!"

His voice raised in a rallying cry. "Do you want an Ashday's Child in your midst?"

As one voice, the massed gathering had thundered back: "No!"

"Do you want a child tainted by the Mark Of Ash?"

"No!"

"Ashday—the time that the ash fell—is a time of evil and wickedness in our history, brought upon our lands by the sins of our forebears from the Old World. Do we want reminders of those dark days?"

Back came the ritualistic response: "No reminders; no Ashday's Child."

Again Jontil shuddered, this time at the memory of how he had cast one of the first stones at his friends' helplessly bound bodies and how he had been amongst those laying burning torches to their hut, razing it to the ground.

As the days wore on and turned into weeks he fancied he heard others whispering and casting furtive glances his way, no doubt wondering why Laoni had started keeping herself out of sight. Ever since Laoni told him they were expecting an Ashday's Child he had despaired that unless they could successfully hide her for the next two quarters they would face the same fate as Brantis and Leila.

And when the baby was born, what then? They would have to hide their offspring, too. Perhaps even kill it. After all, was it not said that Ashday's Children were tainted with the Mark of Ash—an unwelcome reminder of Mankind's ultimate folly, of that time, millennia ago, when their forefathers had caused the deadly ash to descend upon the earth, destroying every civilisation across the globe? That story had been passed through countless generations.

How much longer could they successfully hide their guilt, he wondered...*how much longer?*

* * *

Darkness was fast ending its vigil over the countryside when Jontil joined the throng of men, women, children, and babes in arms, on their way to the weekly dawn thanksgiving. He saw with dismay that Mastron was heading towards him. There was no escape; he was too close to the henge to deviate from his path. Within seconds Mastron was alongside, matching him stride for stride. Then came the expected question: "Laoni not with you again this morning, Jontil?"

"Does it look like it?" he snapped back, keeping his head low to avoid the probing blue eyes.

Mastron laughed easily at the indignant outburst, holding up his hands in mock surrender.

"Okay, okay, we're only concerned because we haven't seen her for a while."

Jontil glanced around cautiously to see whether anyone else was listening, but they were all too deep in their own conversations to take any notice.

"Sorry." He adopted what he hoped was a lighter tone. "It's just that she's still not well. She's a little sick and has the pain of fire around her heart." That last part was true, at least. The morning sickness would have kept her confined to their hut even if their unborn child were not casting a shadow of shame.

"I see," mused Mastron. But Jontil wondered whether he really did. "Tell her from me to get well soon." And with that, Mastron sprinted off to join a group of five friends who were laughing amongst themselves as they trekked through the outer pillars of the henge towards the hallowed ground beyond.

As usual, the crudely-constructed wooden stage on the far side of the area was bedecked with offerings of fruit, vegetables, and salted meat. Today it was the turn of those who had lived between forty and fifty summers to bring gifts. Next week the honour would fall to villagers who had not yet seen twenty-one summers, and Jontil had already put aside a salted loin of cattle to take.

He looked around the throng of people stretching away across the arena, everyone wearing the same type of light brown, shapeless tunic, some barefoot, others with sandals strapped to the knee. And as if that drab costume were not enough of a uniform, almost everyone's hair was raven black, tumbling in thick, cascading waves to their shoulders, male and female alike.

The sun had been above the horizon for several moments already. Its rays were slanting brightly into the henge between the enormous stone pillars, creeping towards the ancient four-branched candlestick. At the exact second the light struck it, the stage-drapes swished aside, their intricately threaded beads clattering against each other, revealing the Star-Gazer and the Holy Man in their full bejewelled glory. The sunlight, ever strengthening inside the henge, accentuated the flashes of red, gold, green, yellow, and blue which zig-zagged across their white, ankle-length robes. The Star-Gazer remained still while the Holy Man took four paces forward and flung his arms wide; pointing his fingers towards the heavens.

He threw back his head, and an ear-splitting roar shot from his lips: "All-Seeing-All-Powerful-One, we give Thee thanks for the dawning of another seven days."

Jontil joined the congregation's response, his voice harsh and raucous in the rhythmic chanting: "Sunday, Sunday, we thank Thee for Sunday."

Like the scores of other villagers in the henge he did not need to think about his role in the weekly thanksgiving ritual. Having taken part every week for as long as he could remember, his responses were totally automatic.

"Sunday, Sunday, we thank Thee for Sunday." This time each syllable was accompanied by a matching-tempo handclap.

"Fireday, Fireday, the time that the world burned.

"Ashday, Ashday, the time that the ash fell."

The volume of the ritualistic chanting increased, as did the tempo, quickly building to a deafening crescendo.

"Sunday, Sunday, the time we saw the sun."

"Moonday, Moonday, the time the moon shone through."

Reaching fever pitch, the crowd, which numbered almost all of the three hundred villagers, whipped into a frenzy; every head slashing the air wildly from side to side as the words tumbled from their spittle-flecked lips—Fireday, Ashday, Sunday, Moonday, representing the four quarters of their year.

Having arrived at its zenith the chanting died abruptly, leaving the clapping to fade away slowly. The Holy Man lowered his arms, his piercing black eyes scanning the villagers. Then he waved his hand across the food beside him.

"Dwellers of Thiecon, the All-Seeing-All-Powerful-One thanks you through me, His Chosen One, for these gifts; the fruit of your labours."

The villagers responded as one: "In return, He gives us life."

Again the Holy Man's arms reached for the skies. "He thanks you for the fruit."

"In return He gives us light," thundered the chorus of voices.

"He thanks you for the vegetables."

"In return He gives us sun and rain to bless the land."

"He thanks you for the meat."

"In return He gives us rest."

"He thanks you for your worship."

"In return He gives us salvation."

"Dwellers of Thiecon, your commitment and loyalty to Him, The All-Seeing-All-Powerful-One, are rewarded. He sends the Star-Gazer to guide you."

"By holy and ancient Thiecon lore He sends the Star-Gazer to guide us."

"He commands that you do the Star-Gazer's bidding."

"We will do the Star-Gazer's bidding."

The Star-Gazer stepped forward to take the Holy Man's place at the centre of the stage. His voice held none of the rich, robust qualities of the one the gathering had just heard, being more of a thin, whining cackle. From Jontil's place at the very back of the henge he had to strain to hear the words. But hear them he must. He could scarcely afford to miss what the day had in store for him.

"For those born in the First Quarter," cried the Star-Gazer, "today gives you the chance to close any outstanding bartering deals, but it won't come easily—you will need to give plenty in return for what you gain.

"Beast keepers beware. Your downfall today will be of your own making."

Jontil gave a startled jump. That was him, a keeper of beasts. The Star-Gazer had spoken, so he must be extra vigilant to make sure things did not go wrong today.

He stared hard at the Star-Gazer. Just how much did he know? How far did his powers stretch? It seemed to Jontil that the noble, hook-nosed head with its iron-grey hair held back in a ponytail, was staring almost hypnotically in his direction. Abruptly Jontil turned his face away, still feeling those jet-black eyes boring through the back of his skull.

That night, Laoni's shallow breathing on the rough sackcloth pillow by Jontil's ear told him she was asleep. He wished he could drop off so easily, but his thoughts continued to turn mercilessly to the increasingly dangerous situation they found themselves in. He wondered whether the village elders would be able to help them. He had heard tales of herbal remedies being able to remove an unborn baby from its mother's womb for the elders to cast into the flames of a sacred fire, so it should have no life of its own. *Maybe tomorrow I'll talk to a village elder, see what can be done.*

Gradually his thoughts became more indistinct, as sleep began to wash over him, drenching him in a dream of villagers screaming that they knew the terrible secret he was trying to conceal.

At first the ungodly sound was just a part of his nightmare. Then he realised the baying of hounds and horses came not from inside his mind but from beyond the walls of his hut. Leaping up, he cast the reed matting from the bed and rushed to the window, pulling aside the covering and peering out into the moonlit night.

It was a full moon, clearly showing that the Destroyers of Evil were abroad, threading their way through the huts.

"Laoni," he screamed, rushing back to the bed and shaking his wife violently. "They're coming for us—the Destroyers of Evil are coming for us! Run, quick, before it's too late."

Instantly she was awake, with raw, savage fear twisting her pert features. Clothed only in their night robes as they were, they fled through the main living area of the hut and out into the moonlight, now turned a fiery orange from the flaming torches held aloft by the Destroyers of Evil, who sat mighty and proud, astride their steeds, surrounding the hut.

Frantically Jontil looked for a way past them, but none was to be had; so tightly closed were their ranks.

"No," he screamed. "Leave us alone!"

Heads began to appear through arches and windows. Heads with leering faces and glinting eyes. Word that the Destroyers of Evil were out must have spread like wildfire through the village. All around, Jontil heard whispered voices getting louder all the time, starting to chant until they reached a crescendo, hypnotically repeating the same phrase over and over: "Destroy the evil, wipe it out. Seek and slay this very night."

Laoni screamed hysterically, covering her ears as if shutting out the mesmeric sound would erase its power and the threat of what she knew was sure to come.

Moonlight flashed off the wickedly sharp spears pointing down at them from the gloved hands of the masked riders, whose capes swirled around the horses' flanks. A tall, snorting stallion moved to one side, making way for a multi-colour-robed figure to step through the gap; a figure with a ribbon holding his iron-grey hair into a ponytail. His eyes bored into Jontil's, then he turned to stare fiercely at Laoni.

"Yes," said the Star-Gazer, his reedy voice straining to be heard above the wild chanting. "This is Jontil and Laoni Almana. The powers of foresight granted to my family for generations through the wisdom of the All-Seeing-All-Powerful-One do indeed show the truth, that this couple are going to spawn a child in the forbidden Second Quarter — an *Ashday's Child*."

The violent, frenzied crowd were baying ever louder for immediate blood, even though they knew their appetites would not be satiated until tomorrow, when the Holy Man and Star-Gazer would invoke the stoning ritual as laid down by the ancient laws of Thiecon.

Four Destroyers of Evil leapt from their mounts and held Jontil and Laoni with powerful, immovable hands. Jontil frantically tried to shake them off, but to no avail. Laoni was now sobbing quietly, her hysteria burned away, almost as if she were resigned to their fate.

But not so Jontil. "You've betrayed us," he screamed insanely into the gathering crowd, writhing in a futile bid to shake himself free.

The Star-Gazer's mouth twisted into a humourless smile, and he struck Jontil viciously across the face with the flat of his gloved hand.

"You speak of betrayal." The words were so hostile, so vicious and fierce, that flecks of spittle flew from his humourless smile. "Your own actions betray you, and in turn, betray all dwellers of Thiecon. Never again shall Mankind taint and blemish these sacred lands."

Suddenly he tore his eyes away, pointing across the plain to the distant towering pillars, just visible in the glittering moonlight.

"Take them to the henge, to the sacrificial cell," he ordered the horsemen. Then he turned to the villagers who were crowding around the little hut.

"Come," he commanded above the din. "We have a thousand stones to find for tomorrow's ritual."

CHAPTER 7

NEW LIVES FOR OLD

FOLLOWING INSTRUCTIONS given before Ashday's Child went to sleep, the computer turned on the lights in his personal compartment at the appropriate moment and activated its voice circuits twenty seconds later.

"Timeshuttle will halt in ten minutes."

Ashday's Child swung himself off the bunk and opened his door into the living quarters at the same time that Caitlin came out of her bed compartment—bed*room* was hardly the word to describe the two, tiny personal chambers at the rear of the shuttle, each containing a single bunk built into the wall, a wardrobe that was full with four hangers in it, a washstand, and barely enough room for its occupant to stand when the door was closed.

"Nearly there," he said, smiling at her as she rubbed sleep from her eyes.

"Nearly *where*?"

"I'm hoping it's a civilisation called Thiecon, way into your future."

"And you know this, how?"

He tapped the side of his nose. "I've told you, if I'm right, you'll know soon enough." He turned from her and stepped through into the control area, sitting down in the pilot's seat and powering up a bank of instruments.

"Warning," said the computer. "Transferring power to navigational array will delay our landing by five-point-two-three-two seconds."

"I can live with that," murmured Ashday's Child, keying instructions into the console. The readouts didn't tell him much. In fact they told him nothing.

"Computer, where are we?"

"Temporal distortion moved shuttle eight miles east-southeast along ley line Epsilon Theta 22013."

Caitlin put her hands on the back of the pilot seat and peered over Ashday's Child's shoulder. "So we're still not far from Knightsbridge and Hyde Park, then?" she asked him.

"Not far from where they once were, anyway," he told her. "But I'm more concerned about our time co-ordinates than our spatial movement. Computer, *when* are we?"

"Insufficient data."

"Your system must have some idea, surely?"

"Negative." The female voice was toneless. "Time movement was across incalculable centuries in both directions. Computation to even estimate our present millennium will take two-point-five hours. Shall I commence calculation?"

Ashday's Child sighed. "No. As long as the information's in your circuits somewhere, we can access it later."

More and more systems came back online as the shuttle's regenerated power transmitted across the total range of its functions. Power level indicators were almost back to normal and the background buzz changed in intensity a fraction, accompanying the marginal swaying and bumping as the vessel finally ended the longest journey it had ever undertaken.

"Well, this is it," said Ashday's Child, more to himself than his companion. Then he stood up and turned to Caitlin. "Let's take a look outside."

In all his travels through the Timeshaft nothing had prepared him for his surprise on opening the shuttle's door. Instead of the finely crafted tunnel walls made from a diotanium alloy, which WorldSave engineers had bonded to the kinetic energy of the shaft's molecular matrix, he saw wire-thin horizontal lines of potent force, faintly tinged with a luminous blue light, forming a humming, living archway around them, stretching as far as the eye could see in both directions.

"This is the Timeshaft itself. Raw power cutting through the centuries."

Caitlin's tones were somewhat hushed as she stared in awe—she was a relatively new recruit: "I don't understand…?"

"This is what the shaft really looks like behind the artificial diotanium skin our technicians graft on to the lengths we travel through," he said. "This is the living, breathing kinetic energy contained within the ley lines—the very essence of time itself."

The air between the dozens of rows of pulsating strands which layered from the ground, arching over their heads and back to the ground behind them, shimmered and waved, slightly distorting the scene beyond. But Caitlin could still decipher it: the blond-haired man and raven-haired young woman who huddled miserably against the stone wall wore nothing but short, sack-like tunics and the only light in their dingy, empty room seemed to come from three torches made of a slow-burning, straw-like substance fastened to metal brackets. The couple stared unseeing, almost as if they had retreated into themselves to avoid a horrifying reality.

Caitlin turned to say something to Ashday's Child, but he was yet to see the young couple. He had turned to stare at the shaft's pulsing barrier on the other side of the shuttle. It bisected the room's rocky wall, dropping to the ground outside it, making the stone appear insubstantial and ghostlike.

"Fascinating," he said. "It shows the different dimensions quite clearly."

She tapped him on the shoulder, pointing to the couple just four metres in front of them. His eyes widened and Caitlin heard a solitary whisper escape his lips: "Mother…"

For a second she didn't think she had heard properly and looked up at him, aghast. But there was no mistaking what he said next, despite the fact that his words were hushed: "Father, is it really you, after all these years?"

Caitlin looked at the young couple on the other side of the shimmering barrier, then back to Ashday's Child. He was slowly fingering his watch, which also acted as the portal key.

"Are you alright?" she asked him, then glanced out at the couple again, but their blank expressions didn't register that they had heard anything.

Without taking his eyes off them Ashday's Child slowly nodded. "I think so." His voice was uncharacteristically shaky and hesitant, almost as if he had been rocked to his very core by what he was seeing.

"You said 'Mother'…and 'Father'…?" Caitlin's question faded away.

Again he nodded. "I think they are…" he whispered. Then, shaking off the mood as swiftly as divesting himself of a hat, he turned to Caitlin with his usual business-like manner firmly back in place. "But there's only one way to find out. Let's go and say hello."

He touched the button on the side of his watch and looked on as the ultra-high-frequency wave disturbed the shaft's wall to pre-set parameters. It pushed the pulsing lines of energy aside, creating a portal three metres high and two metres wide in front of them.

Caitlin saw the couple turn quickly towards the gate with a mixture of fear and amazement crossing their faces. They jumped to their feet, pressing back against the stone wall. It was then that Caitlin saw they were both fastened to the rock by a short length of chain locked on to their right ankles.

Ashday's Child strode through the doorway from the ethereal Timeshaft dimension into the world beyond. Caitlin saw his back shimmering as he went up to the young couple, and although she could hear him speak the words were not totally clear. It was if she were listening from the bottom of a well or the inside of a sack. "Good day," he said to them. "I wonder if I can be of some assistance to you."

The couple cowered up against each other, the man squeezing the girl to him protectively.

"Don't be afraid." Ashday's Child's voice was soothing and low. "I've come to help you."

"Who…who…are you?" stammered the young man. "Where did you come from?"

"More to the point," replied Ashday's Child, "who are you? I hope you're the people I've travelled across centuries to find."

"I'm Jontil Almana, and this is my wife, Laoni."

As Ashday's Child turned to face the portal with Caitlin waiting inside it, she saw a hint of triumph in his smile. And was that a slight tear that shone on his cheek? "My destiny," he said, softly, turning back to look at the couple and noticing for the first time the chains securing them to the stone wall.

"I'll explain later," he told them. "But I've come to rescue you. The All-Seeing-All-Powerful-One has decreed that what you've done is not a sin. Your Ashday's Child is someone to be nurtured and loved, not to be destroyed within his mother's womb before his birth because he is different, or to appease the wrongdoings from ancient time."

He looked again towards the portal. "The laser ray, please. Quickly."

Caitlin was too stunned by what was happening around her to respond as swiftly as she would have normally.

"Caitlin." This time there was a slightly harder edge to his voice. "The laser ray, please."

She shook her head, trying to make some sense of the spinning, incomprehensible thoughts. "Sorry," she replied. "Yes, of course, I'll get it."

For a few seconds she disappeared back inside the shuttle before emerging with a black torch-like device, then stepped through the portal from the Timeshaft dimension into the world Ashday's Child had said was called Thiecon.

He caught the look of terror on the prisoners' faces as they saw Caitlin suddenly appear through the shimmering mass of air. "Don't worry," he told them. "She's here to help you, too." Taking the laser ray, he placed its tip about ten centimetres from the chain around the girl's ankle, adjusting a setting in the instrument's handle. Then he touched an indented red button, shooting a quick burst of brilliant white light, shattering a link of the chain.

The girl looked on in amazement, rubbing her ankle while Ashday's Child repeated the performance on the chain holding her companion.

It was only then that Ashday's Child took time to look around the room. "The sacrificial cell of Thiecon," he muttered. "It's just as you described it."

Catilin knew it would do no good to quiz him further, and, for the moment was content to let her gaze wander around the room, too. It appeared to be hewn from solid rock and was about five metres square. Through the one tiny barred window near the ceiling she caught a glimpse of twinkling stars.

"How did you get in here?" Laoni asked. "Why are you helping us like this?"

Ashday's Child simply smiled. "I'm taking you to a new home," he told her. "Far away from here where no-one will persecute you just for having a baby."

The girl looked across at Jontil, her eyes taking on an excited gleam. "We're going to be safe," she said. "We'll be able to have our baby in peace."

Ashday's Child put an arm around each of their shoulders. "You're about to see and experience something which will be beyond your understanding," he told them gently. "Please don't be frightened." And under his breath he added, "I wouldn't hurt you for the world."

He led them past where Caitlin was standing and paused at the doorway into the Timeshaft. "Through here," he said, "is a pathway leading to a far better place than this. A place where you'll be happy and free to bring up your son without the fear of ancient superstition."

"But an Ashday's Child is a mark of shame," said Laoni.

The old man smiled at her encouragingly. "Not where you're going. Come on, let's be on our way there." The young couple allowed themselves to be guided through the portal and into the timeshuttle.

Caitlin couldn't resist a little experiment. She walked all around the portal, stopping for a second or two where she knew the shuttle would be in the shaft. It was just as if it didn't exist, as if nothing existed except for the cell itself. Other than the shimmering doorway, through which she could clearly see the waiting craft, the Timeshaft dimension played no part in the continuing life of Thiecon.

Ashday's Child's slightly distorted voice wafted out to her. "Come on Caitlin. This isn't our only good deed for the day, you know. We've got some people to rescue in the seventeenth century, as well."

Leaving the sacrificial cell behind her, she used the button on her watch to close the door. The blue-tinged lines of kinetic energy instantly covered the space where the gateway to Thiecon had stood—it was just as if the portal had never existed. The familiar background buzz, ever present in the Timeshaft, was clearly audible, emanating from each strand of raw power and time, as it stretched away through the centuries in both directions.

"Caitlin," Ashday's Child called again from inside the shuttle. "I'm powering up. Don't get left behind."

She took one last look at the nakedness of the Timeshaft, seeing it as she had never seen it before. *It's so beautiful. The very essence of the Earth, and of time itself.* With that thought in mind she stepped aboard the vessel, where Jontil and Laoni were staring in amazement at the wonders around them...the wonders that only a highly technologically advanced age could produce; the sort of wonders that would be lost forever when mankind destroyed their world.

Pressing the switch on the console to close the shuttle door, Ashday's Child swivelled his chair to face Caitlin. "Show them how to work the seat belts, please; we're almost ready to go."

"The chauffeur being chauffeured," she said. "I'm honoured. Are you sure you want the pilot's chair?"

"Oh, I only let you sit here under sufferance, you know. And I did promise you a break. I said I'd take us home, if you remember."

A few seconds later Jontil, Laoni, and Caitlin were safely strapped into the passenger seats forming a row behind the pilot's seat. Ashday's Child brought the navigational system online, downloading the file Dr. Gannaton had transferred from WorldSave headquarters...the file containing the time co-ordinates for Nadia Reeder and Phillip Oatridge. The readout confirmed the file had been accepted, and Ashday's Child hit the Program Execute key.

The shuttle rocked with a faint vibration as it accelerated away from the Thiecon era. It was on its way to the seventeenth century.

* * *

The crackling of flames grew ever louder in Nadia's ear. She squirmed against the tree, rubbing her wrists frantically up and down the bark, mindless of the agonising pain shooting through them—her only concern being to weaken the ropes enough to break free.

A sudden voice cut across her efforts. "What's going on here?" She recognised the voice instantly.

"Lord Berkeley!" she screamed. "Help us. Please help us."

"Your Lordship," began Roger Partridge, "you must—"

"Get them out of there immediately," commanded the Earl of Berkeley. Beyond the rising smoke Nadia could see him rushing towards them, but in her heart she knew the ring of fire was already too fierce for anyone to pass through—either in or out.

Partridge's voice was calm, his words slow and deliberate. "I'm afraid I can't do that, Your Lordship. The Good Book tells us we shall not let a sorceress live. I'm carrying out that instruction." He took hold of Lord Berkeley's shoulders, pulling him away from the spitting flames.

"They're not witches," shouted the earl. "They're travelling players on their way to Southwark."

"Players they may be, but they're witches as well," Partridge insisted. "And they'll burn here on Earth before they face the everlasting fires of hell."

Lord Berkeley struggled free of Partridge's grip and started once more towards the conflagration.

"I'm sorry, Your Lordship, you don't understand. Please forgive me for this." Partridge picked up the heavy stick he had used earlier on Phillip and Nadia, and smashed it down with considerable force on to the back of Lord Berkeley's head. The earl crashed to the ground, unconscious.

"What are you doing?" screamed Miranda, flailing her fists at Partridge's face. "What have you done to His Lordship?"

"What had to be done," he replied with the conviction of a fanatic. "He was trying to save the witches." He shook his head slowly, looking at the unconscious form in front of him. "It had to be done."

"No, no, no," moaned Nadia, slumping into the unremitting grip of the ropes around her chest. A flame licked at the hem of her nightdress and ignited it.

* * *

Ashday's Child powered down the shuttle's main systems and spun the seat round to face his passengers. "Well, we're here."

Jontil and Laoni had hardly moved from their chairs throughout the journey, listening incredulously as Ashday's Child explained how they would trade their old lives in Thiecon for new ones on the edge of Old London—another world, another era.

"You need have no fears about the birth of your son," he told them. "Where you're going no-one even knows about the ancient lore of Thiecon. Your son will grow in strength and wisdom through the years."

"But how do you know all this? Are you a true Star-Gazer?" asked Laoni.

The enigmatic smile that had become his trademark for half a century was the only answer he gave her.

Checking that all but life support and warning systems were offline he opened the shuttle door and stood up. "Let's go and introduce you to your new world."

As Caitlin followed them out into the Timeshaft, the familiar electrical hum hit her ears at once, conjuring up a bluish-tinged image of layers of throbbing kinetic power behind the shining diotanium skin.

Moonlight illuminated the world beyond the portal which Ashday's Child opened using the control on his wristwatch; the world of 18 July 1627, according to the chronometer above the gateway. But that moonlight was tinged with a flickering, ethereal orange glow, and above the humming Caitlin could hear an odd distorted sizzling wafting into the shaft from outside. Suddenly even that sound was eclipsed by an agonised, penetrating scream.

Ashday's Child paused on the threshold, his face frozen with a look of absolute horror and disbelief as he took in the scene playing before him: Nadia and Phillip bound helplessly in the middle of the growing inferno. "Wait here," he instructed Jontil and Laoni, and he ran back inside the shuttle, emerging seconds later with a fire extinguisher.

*   *   *

The scream they all heard had been torn from Nadia's lips as fire bit at her legs. But within her rising agony and the horrifying thoughts of what the next few moments would bring, she saw a bright radiance cut across the darkness behind Partridge and the young maid. And a man's silhouette was clearly framed within that rectangle of lustrous light.

This is it, she thought. *The final delirium.* She twisted her feet through the sticks, but the flames came with her, running tantalisingly slowly along the hem of her borrowed nightgown, almost as if they were reluctant to take full hold. Simply teasing. Hinting of what was to come. Yet still, the heat was intense and Nadia knew that within a matter of seconds the flames would become an enveloping cloak, and the agony would become absolute.

In her delirium she looked again at the shining patch, half-expecting it to have disappeared in the same way the mirage of a life-giving oasis teases travellers in the desert sands. Through the fire's heat waves she could see that the man had now gone, replaced by a young woman who was staring at her, open mouthed.

Nadia glanced across at Phillip to see if he were witnessing the same fantasy, but his head was slumped on his chest and he appeared to be unconscious.

When Nadia tried to take her next breath she found she couldn't. Her lungs strained to pull in air from an apparent vacuum, but only succeeded in producing a harsh grating. Eyes bulging, throat burning from the encroaching fire and the want of air…

The flames seemed drawn to the man who was now running towards her, thrusting a squat, cylindrical object in front of him. The flickering orange harbingers of death bent and twisted as if in the grip of an unseen hand, and then suddenly they disappeared. But as they dipped and turned away from her the air went with them. Nadia felt as if she were in a total vacuum, her confused mind registering that the nightmare of the fire had miraculously gone, while her tortured lungs desperately fought this unexpected new foe.

* * *

Partridge looked on in amazement at the figure who had appeared from nowhere, complete with a magic stick which had literally eaten the entire raging inferno. With a howl, the stablehand hurled himself at Ashday's Child, knocking the fire extinguisher from his grasp. All that was going through his fanatical mind was that the witches had been saved by one of their own evil kind. How else could the fire be swallowed up so easily when it had been about to purge the earth of two more followers of the Prince of Darkness?

He was not to know that the magic stick was a simple gas-exchange diffuser, instantly neutralising the oxygen over a five-metre radius, exchanging it for carbon dioxide. The fire, which seconds later would have consumed Nadia and Phillip, had one thing in common with the human process of breathing—it needed oxygen, and starved of that, it had withered and died instantly.

For all that the warlock appeared to be at least three times as old as Partridge, he had no difficulty in throwing him off.

Miranda made a move to help Partridge, but was floored by Caitlin's lithe form. The time-traveller might only be five foot one, but her intense training made her deceptively strong and agile, and a flying leap was all it took to bring Miranda crashing down.

Caitlin saw Ashday's Child reach for the fire extinguisher, and before Partridge managed to scramble back and hold him in a bear-hug he was able to change its setting and pump oxygen back over the area where the fire had been.

*   *   *

As Nadia's grateful lungs hauled in copious amounts of breathable air she saw the stranger flex his muscles to break Partridge's grip and throw him sprawling to the ground. Caitlin was distracted by Partridge rolling into her, losing her stranglehold on Miranda. Taking full advantage of her luck, the maid scooped up a handful of dirt and flung it into Caitlin's eyes; then without a backward glance she darted away into the thicket.

Partridge adopted the same tactic with Ashday's Child and he, too, disappeared into the wood, while the newcomer uttered blasphemous curses from hell, rubbing the soil from his eyes.

"Help us, please," gasped Nadia as soon as she had sufficient air in her lungs to form words.

Picking up the stick which Partridge had discarded, Ashday's Child beat a path for himself through the circle of smouldering kindling and untied the rope holding Nadia to the tree. She dropped into his arms in a dead faint and he carried her out, laying her gently on the ground beside the Earl of Berkeley, where Caitlin took the ropes off her wrists and ankles while he repeated the performance with Phillip Oatridge.

Jontil and Laoni peered out from the relative safety of the Timeshaft, and then looked at each other. What sort of crazy world had they arrived in? Now they ventured beyond its portal, and bent over the three unconscious forms while Caitlin attempted to revive them.

Seeing the blackened hem of Nadia's nightdress, Ashday's Child swiftly examined her legs where the fire had begun to scorch. Then he spotted Caitlin's concerned look. "They're not really burned — more singed than anything," he said. "But they could still be pretty sore. There's a salve spray in the shuttle which'll take the sting out. I'll go and fetch it."

By the time he returned with the shuttle's small medical kit and started to spray systematically in slow vertical waves, the Earl of Berkeley was beginning to come round, rubbing the back of his head and looking ruefully at the sticky patch of blood that the action left on his hand.

"What's been happening here?" he groaned, looking first at Nadia and Phillip's sprawling forms, then to Ashday's Child and Caitlin, and finally to Jontil and Laoni.

"My friends and I are travellers," began Ashday's Child. "We happened to be passing and saw these two youngsters about to be burned at the stake. Perhaps *you* could tell *us* what's happening?"

"More travellers..." mused the Earl, looking at Caitlin's black leather skirt, black leggings, and heavy boots; then to Ashday's Child's grimy checked trousers, lank, greasy hair and the chin sprouting four days' neglected stubble; and finally to the sack-like tunics adorning the other pair. "Don't tell me you're part of Nadia and Phillip's acting troupe?"

Caitlin looked up sharply and was about to speak, but Ashday's Child beat her to it. "My dear fellow," he said, "the very same. How did you guess?"

"It wasn't difficult," murmured the earl. "Were you abandoned too, or have you come back for them because you're feeling guilty?"

"We...er...we've come back for them." Ashday's Child decided to play along with any line the earl might feed him.

"So you're responsible for the little jest, are you, of taking their luggage and horses and leaving them stranded?"

"Certainly not," retorted Ashday's Child indignantly. "But we did feel we should rescue them."

"Well, your friends nearly lost their lives. I was responding to a call of nature, as I have to do in the early hours of every morning, when I saw the orange glow of the flames through the trees. By the looks of it you only just got here in time to save them...and me. Partridge would have done for me, too, if you hadn't come along."

"So it would seem," said Caitlin, feeling Nadia beginning to stir. "Look, could I suggest that you fetch help while we bring them round?"

"Of course. I'll go and rouse my butler and housekeeper." He disappeared in the direction of the manor.

"He called them Nadia and Phillip," hissed Caitlin, almost before he was out of earshot. "This is who we've come to get?"

Ashday's Child nodded, his eyes flicking from Phillip to Nadia. "Yes indeed. As he said, we certainly arrived in the nick of time. If we'd been just a few seconds later the consequences to the known course of history just don't bear thinking about."

"When are you going to tell me what you're talking about and what exactly is going on?"

A mischievous gleam lit his eyes. "Now's hardly the time. We'd better revive these two before he comes back. We need to get our story straight."

Dipping into the medical case he pulled out another spray, this one considerably smaller than the salve, no more than four centimetres long and tapering to a point at one end, with a small indented button at the other. Putting the tapered tip beneath Nadia's nostrils he thumbed the button. A brief shot of gas ejected with a faint hiss, and Nadia's head rocked back sharply.

"The gaseous essence of ammonia and eucalyptus," explained Ashday's Child.

"Smelling salts," Caitlin interpreted. But Jontil and Laoni retained their blank looks.

Suddenly Nadia was fully awake, staring around her, wide-eyed. She spotted Phillip's prone form and saw Ashday's Child bring him round with another shot from the smelling salts spray. Then realisation dawned that they were safe, and she flopped down on one elbow, looking into Caitlin's face.

"Thank you," she breathed. "You saved our lives."

Caitlin nodded in Ashday's Child's direction. "He did," she told her.

Nadia looked behind Caitlin at the open portal leading into the Timeshaft dimension.

"This is seventeenth-century Old England," she said. "They don't have things like that spray…what's that light and…and…doorway…and how did he put the fire out? I don't understand."

"We're like you," said Caitlin. "Time travellers from the future. I'm Caitlin Lang and my colleague is known as Ashday's Child. We're here to take you back to your timepod in the twentieth century."

Nadia struggled to take in what she was hearing. "But we're pioneers of time travel. Ours is the first trip through time."

Caitlin smiled as she understood the paradoxes that time travel would bring—indeed, had brought. "You are pioneers," she said. "Or rather you *were*, in your day."

"Our day…?" Nadia's tone suggested indignation.

"Yes, your day. The time travellers of my era learn all about your early expeditions in their history lectures."

"History…" This was getting too much for Nadia. "What era are you from?"

"Not too long after you, but long enough for considerable steps to have been made since you began this voyage. Our home is the twenty-eighth century."

Ashday's Child came across to them. "Our young friend Phillip here tells me that the Earl of Berkeley—the gentleman who's gone to raise his butler—very kindly took you in for the night, believing you to be travelling players en route to Southwark."

"It seemed the right thing to say at the time," smiled Nadia.

"Absolutely," he replied. "I heard Caitlin telling you why we're here, but I don't think any good would come of letting the earl in on the secret. It's best if he continues to think we're part of your group come back to look for you.

"And I must talk to Jonathan and Louise before His Lordship comes back." Ashday's Child went across to the young couple who were still staring around in wonder, and began speaking to them in earnest.

"Who?" said Nadia, as a memory began to stir. The memory of a grave in Cranford Park.

"Don't ask," Caitlin replied. "Just don't ask. Actually…" Her voice trailed away. "Jonathan and Louise…?"

CHAPTER 8

MEMORIES

"SO DO YOU GET TO HEAR about politics much on your travels?" asked the earl, as he reached across the dining table and skewered a sizeable hunk of venison with the long, widely spaced tines of his fork.

"A little, now and again," said Ashday's Child. "It's interesting to see how the cultures of one country move to another. Take these forks for example." He held up the ornate silver instrument he was using to eat his venison and chicken. "These originated —"

"Ah," interrupted the earl. "Yes. Forks. Still considered in some parts of England to be a passing fad, and somehow, not manly. We've had them here at the manor since 1612. We all use them here now. That fool, Crosskerry, of course, vehemently opposes them. Says only human fingers are worthy of touching God's food. He was burying one of my staff a couple of years ago, and said his death was God's way of showing his displeasure over the use of such a shocking novelty. Old Barsey was seventy-one."

"I'm yet to be convinced that forks are the work of the devil," said Ashday's Child. "Personally I believe they have a great future. I actually met Thomas Coryate during his travels in Italy in 1608, and he was so enthusiastic about forks."

"Really? Coryate was an associate of mine around that time. That's why I was one of the first houses to take them on. He introduced them to me on his return home in 1611, and I remember how proud he was that I had a complete set of forks when I entertained him to dinner here shortly before he set off on his travels again in 1612.

"Food's changing, too," said the earl. "We always have venison from my estate, of course, and chickens, too. But, tell me, what do you all think of the lamb with artichoke heart and kidneys?"

"Wonderful," said Ashday's Child. "But…"

He spotted Caitlin's astonished glance but was spared having to comment further by Nadia saying she was looking forward to the berries and spiced fruit pies.

Phillip indicated the selection of sweets at the end of the table. "And the syllabub looks delicious."

When the meal was drawing to a close Jacobs stepped forward with a tray holding a decanter and seven glasses. "Brandy for your guests, m'lord?"

"Oh, I think so, Jacobs, don't you, Mr. Strangelove?" said the earl, using the alias Ashday's Child had given to him during their earlier introduction.

"I think I could be persuaded. Thank you very much."

Jacobs poured a considerably generous measure into all seven glasses, and placed them in front of everyone.

As Laoni picked up her glass Ashday's Child looked across sharply at her. "Louise, do you really think you should…?" He pointed to her stomach. "With the baby?"

Her blank look was shared by the earl. "And why not, Mr. Strangelove?" he said. "This is excellent brandy. It'll do her baby the world of good."

Ashday's Child looked across at his mother. His mother! With a tiny foetus in her womb. A foetus that one day in this primitive era would grow into…

Well, into me. A shiver ran the length of his spine. His mind whirled, taking in the paradoxes he was creating here. But his destiny had been sealed long since. *Am I just a passenger in all this?* he thought. *What control do I really have over any of it?*

He smiled. As Ashday's Child moved his leg to get a little more comfortable in the wooden dining chair, he felt the bottle of sweet cider deep in his jacket pocket. *Cider, for quaffing,* he thought. *A world away from this brandy for sipping.*

"Perhaps just this once, then," he conceded, raising his own glass. "*Saluté.* A toast to your baby."

"Nonsense," said the earl. "Louise, my dear, you must have a second glass once you've drunk that. Brandy keeps your spirits up, and keeps you fit and healthy. Your child will grow into a fine young man or woman if you drink plenty of brandy during your pregnancy."

He turned to Ashday's Child. "You must come across plenty of good wine and brandy on your travels. Make sure you keep this young lady well plied with it."

Ashday's Child shuffled a little uncomfortably in his seat and looked at Jontil and Laoni. "Well, now that you mention our travels, I've got a little proposition for you, my lord."

"Ah, now I'm intrigued."

"Travelling is a wonderful life if you're single, like Phillip, Nadia, Caitlin, and myself. And even for a young couple like Jonathan and Louise. But now their circumstances have changed, I'm not so sure the touring life is still right for them."

Laoni reached over and took Jontil's hand.

"I think I see where this going," said the earl.

"Once we've finished our series of performances at the Globe we're making our way back to France and Italy. It's going to be an arduous journey, and even with the copious amounts of wine and brandy that you suggest, I fear it may be too much for Louise."

He coughed. "What I was wondering, my lord, is if you would be able to take Jonathan and Louise on in any capacity, here at the manor?"

For a few moments no-one spoke, each apparently deep in their own thoughts.

Strange how things work out, pondered Nadia. *Just a couple of days ago we were considering asking the very same question for ourselves.*

"Before Jonathan fled the uprising in his home country in eastern Europe he worked on his father's farm," explained Ashday's Child. "He's used to looking after horses, indeed, all manner of beasts. It was only when he met Louise and my touring troupe in Heidelberg that he decided to become an actor." He winked at Jontil. "And a mighty fine actor he is, too."

"Your name, Allman, doesn't have a European ring to it," mused Lord Berkeley. "Where does it originate?"

The earl didn't catch the look of panic which flashed on Jontil's face.

"Indeed it doesn't," said Ashday's Child smoothly. "When Johann Borgemannstein, here, joined my troupe we were on our way home to England, and it was decided he should adopt an English name. After all, who, here in England, could pronounce such a mouthful as Borgemannstein?"

Caitlin simply smiled to herself. Ashday's Child never ceased to amaze her.

The Earl of Berkeley drained his glass, and indicated for a refill. "Drink up, everyone," he said, as Jacobs hovered, decanter in hand. "I think we all have a very important decision to make. Let's sleep on it."

*   *   *

"Well," said the earl over breakfast the following morning. "I do need a new stablehand and maid, now those rogues Partridge and Fengriffen have fled." He looked across at Laoni. "And I do agree, Louise, it'll be better for your baby to be born here than somewhere on the road between acting shows.

"What do you say?"

Jontil touched Laoni's arm tenderly. "I think it's a wonderful opportunity. You know how I'd love to get back to tending animals."

Her eyes shone. "It does sound wonderful, Jonti—Jonathan. This would be a safe place for our baby to grow up."

"And you're not going to be comfortable sewing costumes and making up the actors' faces for much longer," commented the earl.

Jontil smiled. "I think my wife has said it all. It's a wonderful idea for us to stay here. We accept your gracious offer with thanks, my lord."

After breakfast Ashday's Child took Jontil and Laoni for a walk around the grounds, stopping when they reached the site where Phillip and Nadia were rescued from the fire. "I need you to do something for me," he said.

"Anything, Mr. Strangelove." Laoni gingerly stroked his cheek. "You've saved our lives and given us hope for a wonderful future, both for ourselves and our child."

"On your son's twentieth birthday I want you to bring him to this very spot and give him this." He took off his wristwatch and handed it to Jontil.

"You're sure we're having a son," teased Laoni. "I could be carrying a girl, you know."

"Believe me, you'll have a son, a wonderful little boy," smiled Ashday's Child. "He'll be a credit to you, I promise. Now, it's most important that you bring him here on his twentieth birthday. But, here comes the difficult part." He looked into her shining eyes. "Your son's destiny lies beyond that door you came through last night, and I'm afraid you'll have to let him go."

He gently took her hand, then wrapped an arm around Jontil's shoulders, hugging them both tightly. "After his twentieth birthday you'll never see him again." *Until now, Mother,* he desperately wanted to say. *Until now.*

Tears glinted in Ashday's Child's eyes as he watched the happiness dissolve on his parents' faces.

"But...why?" Laoni's voice sounded small and pained.

"Yes, why?" Jontil stared hard at Ashday's Child. "We owe you everything, and you know we'd do anything for you. But to give up our son?"

Ashday's Child wanted to scream out the truth, but he knew he was already creating almost unmanageable time paradoxes, and he felt the effect it would have on this innocent young couple—who were soon to become his parents—would be far too much for them to bear.

His voice faltered, the words choking on emotion. "But know this...he will live for many, many years, and please believe me when I say I know that not a day will go by when he won't be thinking of you. But his destiny lies far beyond that doorway, far beyond this time."

Jontil stared at him, his eyes narrowing. "I hear what you say, Mr Strangelove, but it's difficult for us to believe that you know so much of what is yet to come, and yet you say nothing about why we have to give up our son."

Never before in the whole of his existence had Ashday's Child felt as he did at that moment.

"This is the hardest thing I've ever had to do." He placed both hands on Jontil's shoulders, focusing his weasel eyes squarely on the young man's face. "One day your son will understand. He will know the truth while you never can."

Laoni took her husband's hand.

Ashday's Child turned his gaze to her.

"Destiny plays merry games with us all. It was Destiny's wish for you to conceive an Ashday's Child, and for you to escape your execution in Thiecon, enabling your son to go on to meet his destiny.

"The world will owe your son a great debt; a debt that can never be repaid. For he will save the world many times over. Take that as comfort."

Rippling undercurrents of emotion continued to tug at his heartstrings while he comforted this couple, whom he remembered with so much love and affection from so very long ago. He remembered his tenth birthday, when a happy and proud Jonathan Allman told him Lord Berkeley was going to pay for a private tutor to live at Cranford Park to educate him; how the earl looked upon him as the son he never had; how he started going on the earl's riding parties; how his parents grew more and more strained as his twentieth birthday approached; his happiness when, the day before that birthday, the earl offered him the position of estate manager.

His memory of the birthday itself...

His mother and father were by his bedside when he awoke, and straight after breakfast they took him to the edge of the wood, where more than twenty years ago they had arrived in seventeenth-century England.

"All we ask of you now, my son," said Jonathan Allman, "is that you listen to what we have to say."

The young man had been told many years earlier about his parents' former lives and their rescue from Thiecon, but he was somewhat sceptical about a key opening a special door through time, which he had to pass beyond on this, his twentieth birthday.

"So where is this key?" he smiled, only half-believing that his Father would be able to produce it. But produce it he did. "Mr. Strangelove called it a wristwatch." Jonathan passed it to his son, whose smile now changed from mischievous to quizzical.

Young Ashday's Child turned it over in his hand, fascinated by the strange metallic feel to the pliable strap, and unable to keep his eyes off the ever-changing numbers in a small rectangular box.

"Mr. Strangelove showed me how to unlock the door when the time came, with this device on the side," said Jonathan, and, guiding his son's hand in the direction of the clearing, he pushed the button. The young Ashday's Child shot back in alarm. And as it had been more than twenty years since Jonathan and Louise Allman had seen the entrance to the Timeshaft, they, too, were startled by the sudden appearance of the shimmering portal.

Ashday's Child turned to Jonathan in amazement. "Father, you weren't jesting…?"

"I'm afraid not, my son. The traveller asked me to show you this doorway today, your twentieth birthday and to give you this key with which to open it. Two more travellers will greet you on the other side, if our friend of long ago keeps his word."

"He's kept it, Jonathan," came a young female voice from within the Timeshaft. A voice which sent a thrill of recognition through Jontil and Laoni. "We've come to meet your son, to show him the way to his destiny."

Ashday's Child stared in amazement at the figure which stepped through the doorway to greet him.

"Nadia!" gasped Laoni.

And now, twenty-one years in chronological time before that moment, an Ashday's Child who was more than fifty years older, fought back rising tears while he bade farewell to Jontil and Laoni Almana, standing on the threshold of their new lives as Jonathan and Louise Allman.

Afterwards, he was strangely quiet, and walked ahead, alone, as he made his way with Caitlin, Phillip, and Nadia towards the Timeshaft on the edge of the young wood.

"Before we go in," he said, "I think it's time you all had an explanation."

"And not before time," grinned Caitlin.

"Not before time being the operative phrase." Ashday's Child groaned slightly as he eased himself down on to the mossy grass.

He's aged so much, thought Caitlin. Her memory flashed to her recent conversation with him in a Kensington hotel room—it was only yesterday, but still three hundred years into the future—where he had confessed to getting old and tired. *The great Ashday's Child*, she had said to him. *Never*.

He patted the ground alongside, indicating for them all to sit with him.

"Where does time go?" he asked rhetorically. "Do our actions as time travellers change what would otherwise have happened, or is everything already laid down in a predetermined plan? Well, I happen to believe in both destiny *and* action, my friends. And I do know that I wouldn't be sitting here with you now if I hadn't just given my parents precise instructions on what to do on their son's twentieth birthday—*my* twentieth birthday."

"They were your parents...?" began Phillip, incredulously. "You're the baby she's expecting?"

"But it was purely by chance that the shuttle landed in the sacrificial cell in Thiecon," said Caitlin. "Wasn't it?" she added, a little uncertainly.

His enigmatic smile prefaced the answer. "Was it? That's why I posed the question. During my years with WorldSave I've changed so much of history. Or have I? We've seen the results of my work, and the work of other WorldSave agents in preventing environmental change and disasters. But have I actually *changed* history, or have I simply guided it the way it was supposed to go?

"WorldSave technology can predict alternative timelines, but we're all here, right now, in this timeline reality.

"The beginning of all that's happened, including the creation of the Timeshaft itself, can be traced back to one single, fixed point in time. Without that, I doubt any of this would have come to pass.

"The moment which set my destiny on its way, was the shuttle stopping at the Thiecon cell at the precise time my parents were incarcerated there. That one seemingly random event set off this whole incredible time travel scenario."

He turned to Phillip and Nadia. "And what happens if I don't give you the secret of the kinetic power linking the strands of time, along with the knowledge of how to travel those lines of power, for you to take back and give to TRAEP ten years before your first voyage? Will we still be sitting here?"

Phillip shook his head. "You...give us the secret? I'm sorry, I don't understand."

"You will." A long lingering sigh slipped from the old man's lips as he leaned back on the grass looking at Caitlin. "Despite all our efforts, all the work we've done across the centuries, and no doubt your generation will continue to do long after I'm gone...despite all that, mankind will still lose his domain on this earth. Despite our best efforts he will still manage to destroy this green and wonderful planet eventually.

"We know WorldSave has been able to postpone the moment of ultimate destruction by about twenty-eight centuries, but mankind still, finally, dies in the fiftieth century." A misty look clouded his eyes.

"What about your civilisation, though, Ashday's Child?" Caitlin's last two words sounded odd as they leapt from her mouth. She had known about the man and his daring effort to constantly save the world through the centuries for as long as she had been a member of WorldSave, but this was the first time she had used his alias directly to him in that way. "You told me when we arrived at Thiecon that it was way into the future."

"Ah, my civilisation," he replied with a smile. "Yes, indeed, it's centuries ahead in time, but apart from our brief visit there to pick up my parents" —*or the paradox wouldn't work*, he thought—"we've never been that far through the shaft. It's too far ahead of our own, real time. All we can surmise is that my people developed after your civilisation, which we know wipes itself out."

"So even though we manage to cleanse the earth of nuclear power and the pollution of other dirty energy sources, ignorance eventually triumphs?"

"Not the ignorance that the people of this civilisation were cursed with. Nuclear power, TCR, Rasi-Bisolate, CFC gasses, and global warming were all replaced or corrected. Ignorance comes in many guises—mankind overcame the ignorance that allowed those poisons to emerge and grow. Everything points to another, as yet unknown, man-made catastrophe that finally leads to extinction."

"So our work still holds some meaning?" asked Caitlin, tentatively.

"Our work is the most important ever to be carried out in the history of mankind," Ashday's Child told her. "Without it, none of us would have been born. Civilisation as we know it wouldn't have survived as long as it did—until the fiftieth century—but would have been wiped out at the end of the twenty-second century. My people, of Thiecon, would never have existed, never had the opportunity to rise from the ashes, giving mankind a second chance.

"The central core to all of this is the Timeshaft. Left entirely to his own devices mankind would have destroyed himself around 2,800 years before he eventually does, but thanks to the Timeshaft history took an altogether different path.

"And I'm pleased to say that my work is nearly finished now." Ashday's Child got slowly to his feet. "The circle of time to complete the final paradox is coming to a close at last. There are just two more minor things that need to be done. Let's go and do them."

His right hand reached instinctively towards his other wrist. "Oh, how stupid of me," he muttered. "I won't get that back for another twenty years. Caitlin, will you do the honours, please?"

Caitlin smiled as she hit the button on the side of her watch to create the entrance to the Timeshaft. Instantly the portal appeared in front of them.

Ashday's Child paused on the threshold. "That's why I said I believe in both destiny and action. I'm forced to believe in it," he said, turning to Caitlin; "in my destiny at least. Jontil and Laoni have shown me that."

Taking hold of his hand, she squeezed it gently, trying to use that simple gesture to convey to him that even though she had enjoyed a normal twenty-eighth century upbringing and her parents were still alive back home, she had a degree of empathy with his feelings at that moment.

Looking around at that tranquil seventeenth century scene he began to contrast it with some of the hair-raising escapades he had experienced during his lifetime as a WorldSave agent: the time he was severely injured during a guerrilla raid on a nuclear power plant in the early part of the twenty-first century; the time he was shot while leading an attack on the North Korean presidential palace—he shuddered at the memory of two colleagues being killed on that mission—the time he was badly gored during a Spanish bullfight (and he couldn't even remember now why he was in Spain). His adventures were legendary and legion amongst WorldSave operatives who always listened awestruck whenever his exploits were recounted.

Phillip took advantage of the pause. "What did you mean, earlier, about giving us the secrets of travelling along the time lines?"

"The only way to travel through time is to use this shaft," replied Ashday's Child, pointing to the doorway.

"But we didn't use it," Nadia protested, "and we managed to travel back to the twentieth century in our pod."

"Ah, but you did use it," smiled the veteran. "You just didn't know it." He turned to Caitlin. "Do you see what's happened? If TRAEP had been totally successful in its maiden time voyage we wouldn't have been needed to rescue Phillip and Nadia from this moment in the seventeenth century, and my parents would never have been brought here where I was born. If the pod's drive system hadn't damaged the fabric of the shaft none of this would have happened—that's why TRAEP was allowed to use a substandard propulsion process."

He looked back to Phillip. "We'd never have met you; I wouldn't be able to give you the two data storage keys I've kept in my timeshuttle for the last fifty years; and mankind would have wiped itself out in the twenty-second century."

Phillip shook his head in amazement. "I'm afraid you've totally lost me…"

"I have two data storage keys for you—one for you to give to the twenty-year-old me in the future—your future, that is—and one for you to give to TRAEP ten years before you made, or should I say *make*, your first time voyage." He smiled, enjoying their total confusion. "Don't worry. You'll completely understand in a couple of minutes. Let's go into the shuttle."

He stood at the door, indicating for them all to go through, then he followed them into the Timeshaft.

Nadia and Phillip stared in wonder at the gleaming diotanium tunnel stretching away in both directions as far as the eye could see.

"So this is your Timeshaft, is it?" Phillip's voice was quiet, almost lost to the background buzz of kinetic energy throbbing through the walls into both the past and the future.

"It certainly is. Caitlin…" Ashday's Child pointed to his left wrist. Caitlin closed the portal, instantly shutting out seventeenth-century Old England.

The TRAEP pioneers let their eyes take in the streamlined shuttle parked a few metres along the shaft; the perfectly smooth, curved, shaft walls; and also registered the fact that the tunnel was brilliantly lit, although there were no visible means of lighting.

"Your pod simply latched on to the power generated through the outer matrix," explained Ashday's Child, "rather like a magnet on one side of a pane of plastiglass can hold and move a metal object on the other side."

He reached towards the touch-sensitive pad on the side of the shuttle which would open its door, but his fingers stopped just centimetres from it.

"You know, I'm almost reluctant to give you those data keys. Somehow it'll make me feel mortal again. I've taken too many risks in my career where the odds have been stacked almost impossibly against me, and I've been virtually certain of success, because all the time I knew this day would have to come. But once I give you the keys, that's my part in this time paradox completed." He shivered, violently and noticeably. "See what I mean. Someone's just walked over my grave."

"Well, I know one thing—" began Caitlin.

But he never found out what it was that she knew, because at that moment all four of them were swept off their feet by a sudden swirling maelstrom which struck without warning.

Within a second they had been blasted ten years along the Timeshaft; within two seconds they felt as if every bone in their bodies was being shattered by the unbelievable pressure of the temporal distortion wave; and within three seconds they had, mercifully, blacked out.

CHAPTER 9

BEYOND ETERNITY

WITHIN THE PROTECTION of the Timeshaft the unconscious forms of Ashday's Child, Caitlin Lang, Nadia Reeder, and Phillip Oatridge remained safe from the ravages of the advancing years outside. Lifetimes rocketed by, millennia passed. And inside, oblivious to it all, they slept. Buffeted forwards in time on the crest of a whirling vortex of eddying power, forever feeding on the energy contained within the fabric of the shaft itself, forever growing in strength and in speed.

Were it not for the fact that the tip of the wave curled in front of them to form a natural shield cocooning them from the awesome pressure, their bodies would have been crushed and smashed to smithereens almost immediately. As it was, they were safeguarded in what was the shaft's equivalent of an air bubble in an overturned boat. Bruises and contusions it couldn't prevent, however, and the travellers would be battered and sore when the time came for them to regain consciousness.

Mankind's final destruction came and went before their journey had lasted ten minutes. Man's reign was through, and custody of the planet passed to crustaceans and insects, but as the oceans grew thick and impenetrable, it took just a few centuries for even the hardiest of those living in the water to die out.

On and on they raced until unimaginable aeons of time separated them from anything that resembled the world they knew.

Insects ran riot across the land. What was left of the earth became a seething mass of creeping, crawling life, devouring everything in its path. The insects themselves were only regulated by one form of natural control.

Spiders.

As the very fabric of the earth itself crumbled, the planet's kinetic essence began to seep out through cracks in the ley lines. The temporal glue that held time together was de-bonding.

The different continuum within the ley lines powering the Timeshaft grew increasingly unstable. The turbulence threw the travellers from side to side, until, shortly before the very end of the shaft emerged into the physical reality of the planet's surface, they fell through a widening chasm in the wall. The time energy enveloping them served as their lifeboat. With the laws of temporal physics from within the Timeshaft bearing no relation to time in the outside world, their movement slowed, as almost imperceptibly at first, they wheeled and arced just two yards from the ground.

Tumbling so slowly over and over, still held in the time grip that had come with them from the shaft.

As the two time streams began to merge, they sped up, and crashed down to the rocky terrain. All became still as the dust settled.

Moments passed.

Ashday's Child's age and weariness was truly showing itself. At one time he would have been the first to breach the barrier of unconsciousness, but not now. Phillip had youth on his side and a fierce tenacity of spirit—it was a combination of the two which brought him to his senses first.

His initial reaction to the baleful orange glow bathing not only the sky but the land as well, shot a pang of terror to his heart, sending a surge of adrenalin through his stiff and aching body. *The fire...he was back in that seventeenth-century thicket—being burned by two maniacs.*

As he looked around, though, he realised that nothing could be further from the truth; the world was no longer young. Everywhere smelled ancient and musty, like a long-forgotten tomb. The air hung thick and humid, and suspended in the heavens he saw the source of the strange unearthly twilight. The sun had become a huge red orb, at least three times the size it had been when he had walked with his companions through Cranford Park to the Timeshaft.

But that wasn't all. With the naked eye he was able to see gigantic flares leaping from it every few seconds, for what must have been millions of miles, before plummeting back to be swallowed greedily by the obscene, pulsating mass. Scattered about its surface was a myriad of tiny black dots—tiny from his distance of ninety-three million miles, but he quickly grasped that in reality each one must be thousands of times larger than the earth.

There was no doubt in his mind that its power was waning fast—how else could he stare at it for several moments without hurting and damaging his eyes? Also, its ethereal orange light was only sufficient to dim the stars, not mask them completely, leaving them as tiny pin-pricks of twinkling normality, in the otherwise impossible nightmare he had woken up to.

He was perched on a slight incline towards the top of what appeared to be the only long, sloping hill in sight. All around, the rest of the landscape took the form of jagged peaks reaching out in homage to that waning ball of gas and flame, interspersed with parched and cracked plateaux, but every few hundred metres a small shrub-like thicket grew to about the size of a boxing ring. The plants—if indeed that's what they were—looked dry and reedy; all one colour, a dull greyish brown. There wasn't a hint of green anywhere in sight.

Alongside him Caitlin stirred slightly, before a movement on the horizon caught his attention. Swirling between the gigantic peaks was...*something*. From this distance it was impossible to make out what it was, but as he watched, a dark covering began to blot out the mountains. Its height must have been incredible, because within seconds the entire range was obscured from base to peak. And whatever it was, it was getting nearer.

"Caitlin..." He dug her in the ribs with his elbow and shook her shoulders none-too-gently. The time for awakening her gradually had passed. This coming of rusty-brown tendrils would be upon them in moments.

"Caitlin!" This time there was some response as she rolled over, clutching at a vivid bruise discolouring her left cheekbone.

"Come on," he insisted, shaking her into full consciousness.

"What's happened?" she asked, groggily, pulling herself up to sitting and peering around. "Where are we?"

"I don't know, but we've got to wake the others. Something's coming."

Her eyes widened in terror. "What sort of something?"

He pointed at the mass of fog drifting ever nearer, now only a couple of hundred of metres away, rising up the slope inexorably towards them. "*That* sort of something."

Taking one look at the oppressive swirl, she scrambled to her knees, ignoring the flinty shale cutting through her black leggings, and started gently shaking Ashday's Child's shoulders.

Phillip did the same to Nadia, and within seconds the four of them stood huddled together grimly.

Watching.

Waiting.

As the fog's greasy tendrils swept over them the humidity disappeared, replaced in an instant by a cold clammy darkness, reducing visibility to no more than a couple of metres. And with it came a more powerful version of that musty odour of decay which Phillip had noticed lingering in the air as soon as he had regained consciousness.

"What are we going to do?" cried Nadia.

"We wait for the fog to go," Ashday's Child answered calmly. "Then we try to get our bearings."

"What do you think happened?" Phillip asked.

"Just before we came to rescue you in the seventeenth century we were caught in a temporal distortion which took us thousands of years into the future. We were warned there were probably more of them around."

"What did you call it?"

Ashday's Child looked at Nadia. "A temporal distortion. And you caused it. Or rather, your pod's inefficient drive system did. It's the same thing that snatched you away from the twentieth century and dumped you three hundred years earlier. Goodness knows what era we're in now."

Phillip peered heavenward, unsuccessfully trying to penetrate the chilly blanket enveloping them. "I think I can hazard a guess at that."

Ashday's Child turned an expectant face towards him. "Oh?"

"You probably didn't see it because the fog was on top of us almost as soon as you came round...but the sun's become a red giant, full of sunspots and gaseous flares. It's well on the wane. I don't think there's long left before it dies."

No-one spoke for several seconds. Then Caitlin said thickly: "We're at the end of the world?"

"Beyond eternity," muttered Ashday's Child.

"Everything's gone, then?" Nadia whispered. "Everything we knew?"

"Countless billions of years ago," answered Ashday's Child. "I think it's safe to say this is a very different world to anything we've seen before. You're right about the fog hitting us before I had time to see anything. What are our surroundings like?"

"We're in the open air. It seemed to be halfway up a hill. There was no sign of the Timeshaft. Or your shuttle."

"There could be two possibilities, then."

"What are they?"

"First," answered Ashday's Child, "the hole your pod tore in the shaft's fabric between the seventeenth and twentieth centuries may have become a fault through its entire length, and we've been thrown through it somewhere. And secondly, if the earth is dying here, we could have reached the very end of the Timeshaft."

There was a stunned silence before Nadia asked which he thought was the likeliest.

"I don't know yet." He turned to Caitlin. "Is there anything on the computer?" She pulled a slim handheld tablet from a zipped pocket of her black leather skirt, her fingers prodding gently at the touchscreen.

"I'm getting a very weak signal," she murmured, concentrating hard on the readout. "It's almost as if the shuttle's central core is fading. It could be that the signal's coming from another time, which would mean the shuttle hasn't come with us," she said grimly, before looking up at Phillip and Nadia. "This terminal accesses our shuttle's on-board computer, rather like your time placement recorder taps into your pod's computer."

"You certainly seem to know a lot about our technology," Phillip commented drily.

Ashday's Child answered that one: "As I said earlier, I gave you...or rather, will still give you...that technology. But ours is more advanced, and in theory it means that wherever the shuttle is parked we should be able to use this terminal to access its computer."

"You said 'in theory'?"

Caitlin looked down at her screen. "We've never tried to log on to a shuttle's computer before when we've been in a different time from it, so we don't know whether the signal would register under such circumstances. But I suspect it would be like this. It looks like we've got full access, but response time is very slow."

"Just a thought," Phillip recognised he was probably clutching at straws, "but even if it is a few billion years down the shaft, you can't just whistle it up using that thing, can you?"

Ashday's Child's smile was grim and humourless. "I'm afraid not. All drive and propulsion systems are strictly on-board functions." He turned to Caitlin. "May I borrow it, please?"

His expert fingers flew across the touchscreen, locking onto the co-ordinates of the Timeshaft itself. "The shaft's just over twenty kilometres from here—less than a day's walk. I suggest we make ourselves as comfortable as we can for a few hours and see if this fog'll lift before we try to get there."

"What's the point of going to it if we can't reach the shuttle?" asked Nadia.

"Maybe we can walk down the shaft?" Phillip suggested.

"If we're as far forward in time as we think—namely right at the end of time—it'll literally take us a lifetime to walk back to any period which can sustain life as we know it. And as to the point of us going there, what else do you suggest? We may just strike it lucky and find that the shuttle was washed along with us. We'll never know unless we try."

A frown creased his brow as he keyed in instructions to bring a different set of data to the display screen. "The shaft's energy levels are incredibly high. I've never seen anything like it."

Caitlin peered over his shoulder at the readout. "It's extremely unstable," she agreed. "Where's all that power coming from?"

"Another mystery to be solved when we get there," he said. "But offhand, I'd say it's something to do with those time waves that brought us here."

Nadia shivered, clasping her arms around herself. "This fog's really cold," she said, swirling a hand through it, and watching as a tendril followed her hand's path for a few seconds, like a wake after a boat.

"Yes," said Phillip. "It's not like normal fog at all. It seems more like smoke. Look, it's in waves and strands."

Nadia took another handful, rubbing it between her fingers. "It's greasy." Her voice held an overtone of disgust, and she shuddered, wiping her palm down the front of her silver-grey costume, leaving a dirty smear.

"It's getting colder all the time," said Phillip.

"The fog seems to be thickening," added Ashday's Child as it swirled around his knees, obscuring his feet. "I think we ought to see about trying to light a fire."

"There's nothing here that'll burn," said Phillip, sweeping a small clearing in the swirling mass around his waist. "The ground's almost like flint."

"What about those patches of reeds?" suggested Caitlin, remembering the boxing-ring-sized patches she had seen when first regaining consciousness, just before the fog obscured them. "If we could find one of those perhaps we could make a fire in there?"

"Precisely," said Ashday's Child. "I only saw them for a few seconds and I don't know if they'll burn or not."

"Yes, alright," Phillip conceded. "What was it you said earlier: 'We'll never know unless we try'?"

"Indeed," muttered Ashday's Child, quickly. "Now, the trick is to find one."

"I think there was one about one hundred metres up the slope from us," said Phillip. "We should be able to find it."

Nadia shuddered again. "We need to make sure we don't get separated. I couldn't bear to be alone in this filthy stuff."

"What's that noise?" hissed Caitlin.

"What?"

"Shhh."

"I can't hear anything," said Phillip.

"Will you be quiet," insisted Caitlin. "I heard something moving over there."

They each strained to listen. From somewhere below them a faint scuffle could be heard as if something were scrambling over the loose stones comprising the barren landscape.

Suddenly Caitlin's scream rent the air.

"My leg. Something's bitten my leg. And again. Oh my God, what is it?"

Wafting the smoke-like tendrils aside, Phillip bent to look at her legs, then recoiled in horror. Caitlin's black leggings from her knees to her feet were crawling with all manner of insects: hard-shelled black beetles the size of cockroaches; green, squirming caterpillars, the smallest of which was six centimetres long; small red ants with quivering feelers; but worst of all were the bloated, shuddering, leech-like monstrosities which appeared to have penetrated her leggings and now sunk their sharp tubes into her flesh, drawing blood and causing dark stains to spread out across the material in the second or two before she could react. Then she began beating wildly at the teeming mass of life, knocking dozens off at a time, but making little overall impression on the invasion which crept steadily towards her waist.

"They're on me, too," screamed Nadia.

"They're on us all," Phillip yelled, suddenly noticing that the silver-grey material covering his own legs was rapidly darkening over.

Ashday's Child had been marginally further up the slope than the others, and the insects were only just beginning to climb on him. "Come on, up the hill," he shouted. "They're coming from below us."

Caitlin continued to beat frantically at the relentless hordes and had to be pulled along by Phillip.

"Get them off me," she screamed.

"We've got to get away from them," insisted Ashday's Child. "Otherwise they'll smother us…there's too many of them."

Caitlin snatched her arm free of Phillip's grasp, but the momentum sent her tumbling headlong to the ground, sliding face down into the layer of insects which now covered the shale. She opened her mouth to scream, but a cockroach and caterpillar slithered inside before she could utter a sound. Retching from the pit of her stomach she expelled them before they could get down her throat, and she felt a trace of slime from the insects on her tongue.

Strong arms descended through the fog, hauling her to her feet. Phillip's eyes widened momentarily as he caught sight of the flood of beetles, ants, and cockroaches tumbling from her hair. A leech managed to swing down on a loose lock and anchor itself firmly to her cheek. She tried to brush it aside, but its grip was so tight that she merely succeeded in dragging its needle-tipped tube across her face. Closing her eyes, she slapped her hand hard against its jelly-like body, trying to ignore the squelch as it exploded, showering blood down her jaw and onto her shoulder. The needle sank further into her flesh, as sharp as a wasp sting.

"Come on." Ashday's Child was insistent and urgent.

Phillip scooped Caitlin up into his arms and staggered through the growing mass covering the ground. It was difficult to keep his footing—twice his feet threatened to slide from under him as they crushed insect bodies—but somehow he managed to stay upright, despite being unbalanced by Caitlin's frenzied struggles to brush herself clear.

"Put me down," she insisted. "I'll be fine."

Reluctantly he set her on her feet, and for what seemed like hours, but in fact were only scant seconds, they ploughed on up the slope until the carpet of insects gave way to the flint-like stones once more.

"Don't stop," gasped Nadia from somewhere to their right. "They must be close behind us."

"Quiet," came Ashday's Child voice from about ten metres above her. "I can hear something over here now, too."

"Oh no," moaned Nadia. "They've got us surrounded."

"What the...?" Ashday's Child's words cut off abruptly.

"Ashday's Child, what's happened?" shouted Phillip.

For a few seconds two scuffling sounds seemed to be converging on them in a pincer movement, then Ashday's Child's instruction rang out, somewhat muffled by the fog, which now hung morose and eerie. "Keep absolutely still. Whatever you do, don't move."

"Why, what is it? Where are you?"

"Shut up, Nadia. And close your eyes."

"What?"

"Close your eyes. And shut up."

A black shape, much larger than the insects, brushed past Phillip's legs, then another, and another. And another. Something much heavier and bulkier than the insects clambered up his knee. As he looked down at the newcomer his muscles locked solid and a scream rose in his throat, unable to get out because his jaw was clamped tightly shut and refused to unlock. He tried to close his eyes, wishing he had taken Ashday's Child's advice sooner, but the lids remained steadfastly open. He couldn't even blink. Sheer, undiluted terror paralysed his body in its vice-like grip as the dark shape slowly crawled towards the leech on his stomach.

The spider inching its way across his waist was as big as a blackbird.

Beads of sweat defied the chill in the air, swiftly multiplying on his forehead. Desperately he tried to speak, to move. But the muscle spasm clamped his frame solidly.

In turn the eight legs reached out from the black and orange hair covering the spider's body, propelling it forward at an agonisingly slow pace. For a second or two it stood stock still, as if succumbing to Phillip's paralysis, its knees bent, raising its stomach sac a good five centimetres. Then, as if to prove that size was not the only feature distinguishing it from the ordinary twenty-sixth century spiders that Phillip so loathed and feared, hardened and pointed fangs ejected themselves from both sides of the slavering mouth. He could virtually see the eyes on the ends of the short, stubby stalks, gleaming as the spider sized up her prey.

The movement was so fast it was almost invisible as one of the mandibles shot forward to snatch the leech. A fluid, sloshing, sound hit Phillip's ears as the spider relished her meal. Sweat fell from his forehead, a couple of beads dripping into the striped hair. The stalks moved a fraction in the direction of Phillip's face, homing in on a solitary ant trekking the line of his jaw.

The spider began to inch forward again, continuing her journey. But this time her path took her right across Phillip's pounding heart. It seemed that the spider could either sense, or even feel, the erratically beating organ beneath her feet. One by one the legs came up before dropping back to the same spot. Then, as if to heighten her awareness of each hammer blow, the legs gently stretched themselves out, lowering the stomach sac on to his chest, gorging her sensations on the pulsing beat.

Phillip's adrenal glands worked overtime, and his heart did its best to pump the outpouring of adrenalin around his system, but to no avail; it wasn't enough to lubricate the mental lock with which his arachnophobia secured his muscles.

However, the blood-curdling scream from behind him managed to shatter the lock.

Caitlin had originally obeyed Ashday's Child by closing her eyes. It was only when she felt something crawl off the top of her boot and start worming its way up her leg that curiosity got the better of her. She didn't like spiders, but her dislike was not translated into the absolute horror that Phillip's phobia instilled, so when she opened her eyes and saw the gigantic spider ambling towards a couple of cockroaches which it intended to have for dinner, there was no paralysing muscle spasm; just an ear-splitting scream and frantic swipe of her arm which sent it spinning away.

Snapped into action, Phillip flung back his head, lashing out with his hand. The fraction of a second his knuckles were in contact with the warm fur caused his stomach to lurch, and he fled blindly through the fog.

"No," shouted Ashday's Child, urgently. "Leave the spiders alone. They'll get the insects off us."

An hysterical cry from Nadia: "What spiders?" She, too, opened her eyes just in time to catch sight of one of them devouring dozens of ants which were trying to flee for their lives off her boot.

Then a faint rumbling began in the distance, rolling nearer with alarming speed. And with it came a fast moving ripple along the shale, causing the travellers to stumble violently.

Instantly, the squirming, living carpet around their feet seemed to flow away in much the same fashion that a wave washes back from a shoreline into the sea; the insects going one way, the spiders another.

A sudden tremendous roar away to their right drowned out the growing rumble which had penetrated the fog's eerie deadening effect.

And after the roar, another altogether more terrifying sound could be heard, increasing in power; a cracking sound which made the very ground beneath them shake as if in fear.

"Earthquake," yelled Ashday's Child. "Get down." He flung himself headlong to the ground, rolling into a ball as the land heaved

and rocked. Ashday's Child had been in an earthquake once before—
when the San Andreas fault finally devastated the American coastline
from San Francisco to Los Angeles in 2045—and he recalled with
perfect clarity that same cracking and bucking of the land as a web of
chasms, each almost a kilometre wide, ran between the two cities and
out towards Death Valley. When the dust had finally settled, an area
nearly two hundred square kilometres was criss-crossed with canyons.

That was the noise Ashday's Child heard now, and the dilemma
was made even more acute because they couldn't see where the
cracks were forming. All they could do was hear them as the ground
ripped asunder somewhere in that cloying, clinging blanket of fog.

As stillness eventually calmed the land and quietness returned
to the air they noticed a different quality about the fog. Its tendrils
were now carrying particles of dust which stung their eyes and
belaboured their breathing.

"We've got to get out of here," said Nadia, before a dust-induced
choking cough strangled her words.

"We're not going anywhere until the fog clears." Ashday's
Child's voice came from a little way off, and his words, too, were
interspersed with coughing. "We must stay in a group. There's no
telling where the quake has opened cracks in the land. It's too
dangerous to move while we can't see more than a metre in front of
us. I'll keep talking so you can find me."

Caitlin and Nadia were with him in a couple of moments.
"Where's Phillip?" he asked them. "Isn't he with you?"

"He helped us when we were attacked by the insects, but I've no
idea what happened to him after that," said Caitlin.

Calling him proved fruitless.

"We've got to find him," insisted Nadia.

"Of course. And so we shall. But not until this fog clears,"
Ashday's Child told her firmly.

"But when's that going to be? We've no idea how long fog lasts
here."

No-one spoke for a few moments. Eventually Nadia broke the
silence. "This could last for days, you know."

"You know what they say about crossing bridges," retorted
Ashday's Child.

"And I know what they say about burning bridges, too. Do you really think there's a way back?"

"Talking of crossing and burning, Caitlin and I have crossed centuries to find you and Phillip, and I have a burning sense of my own destiny which isn't going to be denied. We're getting out of this, we're finding the Timeshaft and going home."

"Just what is the Timeshaft, anyway?" asked Nadia. "From what I can gather it's like a tunnel that connects—"

"Caitlin," interrupted Ashday's Child, "why don't you explain to Nadia. Let's see how much went into that noggin of yours during your training."

"Okay, I'll tell it as simply as I can," said Caitlin. "Basically, it's a shaft that runs from the start of time, right through to the end of time. It exists outside normal time and space, and outside the laws of physics. It inhabits..." She thought back to when she walked around the portal in the Thiecon sacrificial cell. "I suppose you could call it another dimension, which is part of the earth, and yet, completely separate. Don't ask me any more, because I don't know. I travel to both my own past and future in it. As to how it works, though; well, that's still a mystery to me."

"But where did it come from?"

"Ashday's Child and I actually travelled to 2345 to create it. We engineered...well, Ashday's Child did...a massive explosion which channelled untold energy into the earth's ley lines. Do you know what ley lines are?"

"Vaguely, yes. Aren't they straight fault lines in the earth's tectonic plate?"

"That's the scientific explanation that the world believes, yes. The world also knows of the powerful electro-magnetic forces generated in these lines. But what only we know, is that the energy connects every point in time through Earth's existence and WorldSave has the means to access that energy and use it for time travel."

"But from what you've said it didn't exist before 2345. If it was only created then, how can you travel backwards in time beyond that point? I can understand you being able to travel forwards. But how could you use the shaft to come to the seventeenth century to rescue Phillip and me? The shaft didn't exist in the seventeenth century."

Ashday's Child cleared his throat. "Okay, Nadia, Look at it this way. If we hadn't created it in 2345 by causing the Australian explosion, it wouldn't exist. But WorldSave has been using it for years. Therefore, it does exist. Which means we simply had to create it. If we hadn't done, then none of this would have happened. Are you with me so far?"

"Yes, I can see that. Sort of. But how can you travel backwards in time to a point before it existed?"

"As Caitlin said earlier, the Timeshaft exists outside the normal parameters of time and space. Both its creation, and how WorldSave came into possession of the knowledge of its quantum physics, are what is known as a causal loop."

"A what?"

"A causal loop. It's a time travel paradox, when a future event is the cause of a past event, which in turn, is the cause of that same future event. I went to the past to create the Timeshaft, which gave me the means to do exactly that. Both events exist in the space-time continuum, but which was the cause and which was the effect? We can't determine the origin.

"And the quantum physics of the Timeshaft are such that it exists in every single point in Earth's time. We're able to access and leave it at any one of those points. The only restriction we have is dictated by the physical presence of the ley lines. Which, as you rightly said, are fixed, straight lines in the tectonic plate.

"Incidentally, Caitlin, I know you've never asked, but you must be wondering why we had to use conventional transport to get from London to Austria in 1994?"

"Never really thought about it. I assume it's because that's the nearest ley line?"

"Well, yes and no. There are still many things we don't understand about the ley line network. There are a few 'island' networks, that don't connect to the main system giving access the Timeshaft. We can't get into the lines covering the part of mainland Europe that includes Germany, Austria, and Switzerland. So, no, it's not the nearest ley line to where we wanted to go, but yes, it's the nearest one we could use.

"This very fact that there's so much we don't know about how the Timeshaft operates within the ley lines gives me hope—no, it's more than hope and its more than confidence; it makes me certain—that we're going to get home. Many causal loops are at work here. Balls are already rolling which I suspect were begun in the future, not in the past.

"And one of those balls is Phillip. Let's just say that I'm convinced he has a part to play in the future that led to the events of the past. So I wouldn't worry too much about him, Nadia. Once this fog's cleared I'm sure we'll find him.

"Now, if you'll excuse me, I want to get some sleep so I'm ready for the exertions ahead, when we make our way to the Timeshaft. It's a long walk. And I'm an old man."

* * *

"Look. Something's happening." Caitlin was right. The dust-laden tendrils which had lain heavily over the land began to swirl again. Each one formed its own little whirlpool and drifted off towards the mountain range. With the fog's departure, the humidity returned immediately.

And what a changed landscape it was, in that oppressive orange twilight, which met their eyes. They were still half-way along a sloping hill, but a new mountain had sprung up less than three kilometres away, with dozens of cracks radiating out from it, the nearest one just biting a fraction into the base of the hill on which the travellers now stood.

And blotting the entire expanse of shale: smaller peaks—many no higher than three or four metres—each jagged and sharp, illuminated by the fiery orange glow.

"What incredible pressure must have been generated to push the land mass up like that," commented Ashday's Child. "And the substrata must be considerably weaker in this era, for just small pieces of land to be affected in this way."

"Like crumpling a piece of paper," muttered Nadia.

"Exactly. The planet's death throes are pretty advanced."

"Death throes?"

"Yes, there are precious few tomorrows for this ailing world of ours, I'm afraid."

Nadia scrambled to her feet. "Hadn't we better try and find Phillip and get to the shaft quickly? At least we can walk a few years back in time…to somewhere where we'll be safe."

"Ah, the death throes will take a little while," said Ashday's Child. "You needn't worry about the earth blasting itself into millions of pieces just yet. I was referring to 'precious few tomorrows' in geological time. I reckon there'll still be a few millennia left." He cocked an eye at the baleful orange ball above them. "Our poor old sun's aged considerably. It's become a red giant, and will eventually burn itself up. But, yes, it'll be there awhile yet."

Caitlin had already walked further along the incline, checking readouts on her terminal. "The Timeshaft's energy levels are still very high," she said. "It seems fairly consistent, though, and it's definitely in this direction."

"Right," he called up to her. "Phillip can't be far away, there's not an awful lot of vegetation to conceal him."

That was an understatement. Apart from the patches of reedy shrubs, the ocean of nothing but broken shale extended to the base of the innumerable peaks. The only respite to that stark geography was the new fissures littering the landscape in every direction.

Ashday's Child spotted Nadia looking at the gaping crack which had appeared a few hundred metres below them while the fog had masked the process. "I shouldn't worry too much about that," he said. "I'm sure if he'd fallen into that crack we'd have heard him yelling."

"Then where is he?"

"We'll—"

Caitlin's call interrupted him. "Ashday's Child, up here, quickly." She stood a couple of paces inside a patch of the reedy growth, peering down at the ground.

"I'm registering minute amounts of kinetic energy here," she said as he came to her side. "And look at this."

She indicated a dark hole, camouflaged to a certain degree by a few of the taller reeds which had flopped over its jagged opening.

Nadia arrived alongside them. "Kinetic energy?"

"It can only come from the Timeshaft," nodded Ashday's Child, peering at Caitlin's readings. "There's no interruption between the energy flow and these traces here. But why didn't they register before?"

"They're too faint. They only show when the input sensor is pointing directly at the hole."

"So could this hole lead us straight to the shaft?" he asked.

"It's possible," agreed Caitlin.

"But it's definitely not a ley line?"

"No. These traces are only residual energy. A ley line, taking us straight into the Timeshaft dimension, would register at least as powerfully as these other readings from twenty kilometres away—if not more so."

A thought struck her as she gazed at the data scrolling across her screen.

"Ashday's Child?" she mused, tentatively. "What are the realistic chances of the shuttle having come with us in that temporal wave?"

"Truthfully…very slim, I'm afraid. The molecular density of a parked shuttle is totally different to the molecular density of a shuttle in the process of using the shaft's kinetic energy for propulsion. The wave carried our shuttle to the time of Thiecon because we were already moving…already merged with the shaft's actual living matrix. A stationary shuttle would be a dead weight and a dead entity as far as the energy from the wave was concerned. No, our shuttle will still be where we left it in the seventeenth century."

"That's what I was hoping you'd say. You know what you said about not knowing everything about how the Timeshaft operates within the ley lines…" A faraway look crept into her eyes as she keyed another request into the tablet. Nodding with satisfaction at the answer, she looked up at him, smiling. "According to this, when we get to the shaft we should be at the same physical location in space as we were when we left the seventeenth century."

Ashday's Child nodded, but couldn't foresee the point she was coming to.

"We left the shuttle for two weeks at the Hyde Park portal in twentieth-century Old London while we handled the Austrian TCR case," she said.

"Yes…?" Slow, long and drawn out: *Yyesss*.

"Would it still have been there if we'd left it for...say...two years of 'outside' time?"

"Of course. It..." Realisation washed over him in a flurry. "Caitlin," he shouted, flinging his arms around his astonished companion. She had never seen him display such an outgoing emotion before. "I love you. You're wonderful."

"Would someone mind letting me in on the secret, please?" Nadia sounded a little irritated.

"Yes, indeed," said Ashday's Child, excitedly. "What Caitlin's saying is that our timeshuttle could have stood at the same gate in physical space ever since we left it there in the seventeenth century, waiting for us throughout eternity. The shuttle could be just twenty kilometres from here."

Nadia shook her head. "It can't still be there after all these billions of years, surely?"

"Why not? Where would it have gone?"

"Well, someone else could have used it."

"Not if we get it back now and return to our own time in it. It's a causal loop paradox, but a perfectly feasible one."

"And what about its condition? Just supposing it is still there, won't it have fallen to pieces?"

"Diotanium alloy? Never. It'll be as good as new."

"Okay, how about its power supply and equipment? Will it still be functional?"

"Without human presence on board for more than twenty-four hours the computer automatically shuts down all systems. The shuttle will be hermetically sealed, so hopefully nothing's decayed. And it draws its power from the Timeshaft's own kinetic energy matrix." He tapped Caitlin's computer screen triumphantly. "And this tells us there's still a vast reservoir of power in the shaft waiting to be tapped."

"So we really could be going home?" Then Nadia's smile disappeared. "But we've got to find Phillip."

Caitlin surveyed the desolate, perpetual twilight landscape all around them. "Phillip!" she shouted.

Suddenly her ears picked up a faint scuffling which sounded as if it came from inside the hole. "What's that?" she hissed, peering into its darkness.

Ashday's Child pulled a pencil-thin torch from his pocket and shone its powerful penetrating beam from side to side in a wide arc. Wherever its ray of light fell, it revealed one of the orange and black spiders. He thumbed a switch on the side of the torch to widen the beam to maximum. The hole itself appeared to be about five metres deep, opening out into a vast cavern on one side. Not a centimetre of ground was visible within it. Everywhere the travellers looked was swarming with the huge spiders which had become their unwitting allies against the ravaging horde of insects five hours earlier.

Caitlin swallowed nervously. "And there's me thinking we may have been able to get to the shaft through here." She recoiled in horror. "Guess we'll have to take the pretty route after all."

A weak cry floated up to them from within the chamber. "What's that?" hissed Ashday's Child, swivelling the torch.

Nadia caught his look of horror as the arc of light found its target. She swung her gaze to follow his frozen stare.

All that was visible of Phillip was his pale, ghost-like face. The rest of his body was cocooned securely in white fibrous strands, some of which were still being spun by a dozen or so spiders.

His voice, when he could finally coax it into action again, was croaky, but imploring. "Help me."

Ashday's Child's reverie was not even broken when a spider's legs appeared from the underside of the hole, levering its obscene body out on to the surface.

Then came another.

Then another.

And another.

CHAPTER 10

A SUMMER BURIAL

14 JUNE 1649

The Reverend William Crosskerry made the sign of the crucifix over his heart and turned from the two open graves to face the assembled group of nine people: the entire household of Lord Berkeley's estate at Cranford Park.

"And so we commit the bodies of our beloved brother Jonathan Allman and our beloved sister Louise Allman to the ground; ashes to ashes, dust to dust. Man, who is born of woman, has but a short time to live upon this earth.

"It was the fate of our dear friends Jonathan and Louise to depart this life before their allotted threescore-years-and-ten.

"How fickle is the hand of time. Had but another second elapsed, giving Jonathan the chance to escape the flying hoof of that runaway horse four days ago, he would have still been with us today. And Louise, seeing the battered body of her loving husband, collapsed and died of a broken heart.

"Jonathan and Louise lived amongst us for twenty-two years, enriching the lives of everyone they knew. Not a happier, content, nor more helpful couple could be found anywhere in London.

"When they came amongst us Louise was with child. Their son, also named Jonathan, was born during their first Christmas at Cranford Park. It was to their credit that they brought this young man up in the manner they did. And Lord Berkeley took to the growing youngster as if he were his own son..."

At the front of the group the Earl of Berkeley bowed his head slightly. "...educating him, offering him a future as his estate manager." The vicar's next words were thunderous and accusing. "The boy flung all this back in their faces. It's little wonder that Jonathan had no fight left in him for survival after that crushing blow to his skull from a maverick horse. I say to you, my friends, that Jonathan and Louise Allman would still be with us today if it were not for the selfish actions of their only son, Jonathan, who chose to leave his parents on his twentieth birthday and seek his fortune overseas.

"The earl's supreme efforts to trace the boy during the last eighteen months have met with failure. Jonathan Allman the younger has vanished off the face of the earth.

"The Lord shall judge Jonathan the elder, and Louise, as loving, caring people who would help anyone, no matter the cost to themselves.

"Their absent son, Jonathan the younger, how shall he be viewed on that dreadful day of judgement when God calls all his subjects before him? A youth who took the best years of his parents' lives before abandoning them. Jonathan the elder and Louise were approaching their middle years, no doubt looking forward to the autumn of their days upon this earth with the love of their solitary offspring to comfort them.

"Let the lives of Jonathan and Louise Allman be a warning to those present today that no matter how you bring up your children, if they are so minded they will simply abandon those they love to pursue their own sinful pleasures.

"Jonathan and Louise did everything they could for their fellow human beings. Jonathan the younger did nothing for anyone, except himself.

"Our dearly departed brother and sister were put upon this earth for the benefit of mankind. What can a worthless person like their son have been created for?"

No one at the graveside saw the middle-aged figure concealed behind a yew tree. The figure in a grey coat which had clearly seen better days. The figure with a face just beginning to form lines. The dark hair flecked with grey, desperately in need of a wash. The narrow, tapering chin desperately in need of a shave.

The figure taking a swig from a brown bottle.

The figure wiping tears from small, weasel eyes, set too close together.

The figure now turning away, with thoughts of an unstoppable destiny firmly ingrained in his mind.

CHAPTER 11

SUNBIRTH

CAITLIN AND NADIA STOOD TRANSFIXED, staring at the hole, watching spider after spider emerge on to the surface, but it was finally Caitlin who broke from the hypnotic spell as dozens of the orange and black creatures swarmed towards them.

She grabbed Nadia's sleeve, pulling her back a few paces down the slope. Ashday's Child, meanwhile, stood frozen as the spiders found his legs and began their ascent.

She looked down at the i-tablet in her hand. It gave her an idea for something the spiders might not like. Turning the input censor to maximum she opened all output channels. Instantly the computer converted its audio input into electronic impulses, sending them through the external speakers as pure white noise. That white noise was sucked back into the system through the intake sensor, converted again, and sent back out. On each cycle the frequency level rose. At first it was merely irritating to human ears; then it became painful, before finally disappearing off the top of the megahertz scale.

Caitlin and her companions could sense it. They knew something was there, something disturbing their inner equilibrium, something reaching directly into their brains.

But it was an altogether different story for the spiders of this dying world. Their highly evolved neural sensors were on the verge of exploding as the ever-increasing pitch tore into them, straining them beyond endurance. Their telepathic communication system became too disturbed for any coherent messages to get through. Each spider suddenly found itself the master of its own destiny, experiencing an unknown feeling. No longer controlled from the central nest, each individual entity found its own personality—a personality restrained from the time of its hatching—no more knowing what to do with its newfound freedom than it would have understood the timeshuttle's complex instrumentation panels had it found itself in the pilot's seat.

Neural control of the invading wave was instantly broken. Those spiders on Ashday's Child's legs lost their grip, falling to the shale, joining their comrades in running in endless and pointless circles.

The torch beam, now shining in an arc into the hole, showed that the spiders down there were not affected as badly as those on the surface. Anarchy ruled...but the downside was that the dozen or so drones finishing off the cocoon holding Phillip prisoner decided to keep their meal for themselves. And they were hungry now.

Ten of them stayed on the ground, fighting off any attempt by their former colleagues to storm their position, while the remaining ones severed the loose strands of cocooning web and began the slow climb up Phillip's immobilised body, sensing that the jellified eyeballs would be as good a place as any to start their meal.

Inside the cocoon Phillip could barely even flex his fingers. Adrenalin, giving the power of fight or flight, had just about drowned his bloodstream in a futile attempt to ward off the constant horror ever since he succumbed to the spiders. Within seconds of his dash through the fog he had been overwhelmed by them, tumbling headlong into the advancing army.

An army that truly marched on its stomach.

The collective consciousness had a predetermined time for forages amongst the insects to collect food. Once the fog dispersed the insects would return to their lair. Some individual gorging was allowed, but in the main when a drone captured an insect it had to return with its prey to the nest.

Never in their race memory could the spiders recall such a gigantic catch, nor one which had fallen into their clutches so easily. The insects thrashed and fought, but always succumbed to the pointed mandibles injecting a paralysing fluid into the victims, which were then cocooned in the powerful strands of web spun from the spiders' bodies, and carried aloft to the underground nest. That same fate had befallen the fleeing Phillip: once the spiders had covered his body all attempts at escape finished, as his phobia launched its immobilising muscle spasm again, combined with the poison from the bites of a dozen drones.

Caitlin pointed the terminal into the hole. The ever-heightening frequency meant the spiders inside the lair were swiftly affected in the same way as those on the surface. Wave upon wave of ultrasonic sound battered them at an intolerable level. The two climbing Phillip's cocoon lost their grip and fell to the ground, running in circles in their insane, futile bid to escape the penetrating power.

Caitlin grimaced as the pressure built inside her own head. She knew they wouldn't be able to stand it much longer, and wondered what retaliatory action the spiders would take when it was turned off.

"Nadia, Ashday's Child—don't just stand there. Get Phillip out. Quickly!"

It was the spur Ashday's Child needed to remind him of his destiny. *The circle must be closing now,* he thought. He hadn't come so far, spent so many years travelling through the Timeshaft for it all to come tumbling down now. If he failed, would any of them even be here? Would the Timeshaft have been created? Would mankind's civilisation have died out in the projected alternative timelines? He had shouldered the responsibility for so long. The call of destiny was suddenly strong again and surging through his every fibre, prompting him into action. Reaching into one of his seemingly bottomless pockets he brought out another torch-like instrument, its radius about six centimetres. Aiming it into the hole he squeezed a trigger and a coil of thin nylon-coated wire instantly shot out, its end disappearing into the darkness.

"Right," he said, thrusting the device into Nadia's hand. "Hold this. I'll go and get him." She fastened the cord around her waist; Caitlin also wrapped it around her own waist and planted her feet firmly into the shale while Ashday's Child swung himself over the edge and shinned down the line to the firm ground inside the hole. On the way down, his weight pulled Nadia and Caitlin a little nearer the hole, but their combined power was enough to hold him until he reached the bottom.

"Thank goodness," moaned Phillip, weakly, as Ashday's Child swept the hungry spiders aside and pulled yet another instrument from those pockets. The laser cutter sliced through the cocoon's steel-like web strands in an instant, weakening it enough for him to lever it open. Phillip stumbled out into Ashday's Child's arms.

A spider ran blindly across his boot and he lashed out in a violent frenzy sending it crashing into the cavern wall.

Ashday's Child guided him to the rope. "Can you climb out?"

"I'll try," said Phillip, looking up at the ring of orange twilight. "It's not far." He put faltering hands on the cord and slowly and painfully dragged himself up, with Ashday's Child pushing from below.

As soon as Phillip was safely out, Ashday's Child scrambled back up the rope, acrobatically swinging his legs out of the hole first, his chest and head appearing upside down in the next second.

"Not bad for a seventy-three-year-old," he grinned, climbing to his feet and dusting himself down. "Come on. Let's get out of here. Now, which way is the Timeshaft?"

The journey was heavy going. Even on the flat land their feet often threatened to slide from under them in the flinty shale. It was only the thought of the fog returning, bringing with it the insects and spiders, that coaxed their aching, exhausted bodies along. For almost five hours they stumbled through the permanent orange dusk, and it was only then that Ashday's Child noticed the sun hadn't moved in the sky.

"It looks like the earth's stopped spinning on its axis," he muttered. "This side of the planet must be in constant light—"

"—and the other side in constant darkness," Phillip finished for him, shuddering at the thought of the insects and spiders having a free reign. "It's a good job we didn't land on that side."

"I wonder if that's where the fog comes from," said Nadia.

"Talking of which…" Caitlin's voice was rising in pitch. "Look over there." Their horror-struck gaze followed her pointing finger to the swirling, greasy tendrils worming their way swiftly between a couple of the jagged peaks which still littered the landscape between the fissures.

Instantly Phillip froze to the spot, his arachnophobia entering the first stage of transforming his body into an immobile mass.

"Right." *This is the Ashday's Child of old,* Caitlin noted. There was no mistaking the power and authority contained within that solitary word. In her eyes his enigmatic character was returning to its true form, despite the recent glimpses of its mortality and humanity. And she wouldn't have it any other way.

He glanced at his left wrist before an exasperated mutter escaped his lips. "I'll never get used to not having my watch. Caitlin, how long is it since the fog disappeared?"

She glanced at her own wrist. "Five hours."

"And I seem to recall it was with us for five hours. It must come in mathematical cycles. Anyway, I think we know how to handle it now."

"Do we?" said Phillip, through clenched teeth.

"We sure do." Caitlin pulled out her i-tablet.

"We can't stand that for five hours," protested Nadia.

"Not at the levels we used last time," admitted Ashday's Child. "But if we have the settings on low it'll simply keep them at bay. I hope. Shouldn't it, Caitlin?"

"It should. It'll act like a force field to keep the insects and spiders out, and won't affect us too much. It could be a little uncomfortable, that's all."

As she adjusted the controls the white noise grew constantly, until it reached the top of the scale audible to human ears. "Now," said Caitlin, keying in a new set of instructions on the touchscreen, "if I set it to drop one cycle of frequency on every intake until it reaches a certain level, then get it to start the process again, it'll stay constant. There. That should do it."

And it did.

For the next cycle of fog they stayed huddled together on that vast plain, resting and chatting. Even Phillip managed to relax, despite the fact that they could hear the terrifying sound of the battle between insects and spiders being fought all around them. Once a spider strayed beyond the audio force field and skirted Caitlin's boot. But before she had time to react the inaudible white noise did its job, sending the spider scuttling back to rejoin the ranks of its colleagues.

"One thing I've got to ask, if you don't mind?" Caitlin's voice came through the fog.

"Fire away."

"Not you this time, Ashday's Child. Phillip, Nadia...what training did you have to do for this mission?

"What training *didn't* we do?" replied Nadia.

"I'm just wondering if it was similar to WorldSave's training. That was pretty hard."

"Hhmmph." Ashday's Child sounded slightly muffled; he had settled down a little further away, claiming again that he needed to sleep. "You youngsters have it easy."

"Thought you were asleep."

"How can I sleep with you lot prattling on all the time?"

"Well, go on, then," challenged Nadia. "Why do we have it easy?"

"No, you convince me why you have it hard. What made a time traveller in your era?"

"Nadia and I both studied astro-temporal physics at the Central Academy of Greater England. It was a four-year course, and our last eighteen months were sponsored by TRAEP. At that time we hadn't heard of them, and our sponsorship came completely out of the blue."

"Why did you get the sponsorship?" asked Caitlin.

"TRAEP said they wanted to sponsor two students and asked everyone in the course to apply. We were chosen. Which was a bit of a surprise as we weren't the top students. We didn't think we stood a chance.

"Anyway, we were told that a condition of the sponsorship was that we'd be trained for a practical time trip."

"And that was something we just didn't think was possible," said Nadia. "But we agreed to it, and duly finished our course. We graduated and joined TRAEP full time."

"Which was when our training began in earnest," continued Phillip. "We were flown to a site in Mexico for what they called Stage One Fitness Screening. For seven days we filed through a maze of laboratory tests. Heart, liver, brain, kidneys, spleen, eyes, ears, even nose and teeth were all checked and double checked. Then our heart functions and lungs came under even more scrutiny, and finally, stress."

"God, that was the worst part," said Nadia. "We were whirled in a centrifugal device until we lost consciousness; blindfolded and put in a vibrating chair, almost until our teeth rattled, and our task was to keep the chair upright. Then we were locked in a darkened, padded room for three hours before being transferred to a chamber for two hours where the temperature was 122 degrees Fahrenheit."

"Those are just the physical tests we're allowed to talk about," said Phillip. "Many are covered by the Official Secrets Act, and I'm afraid we can't tell you anything about those."

"Similar to some of my training at WorldSave, before I was cleared for time travel missions," said Caitlin.

"Really?" Ashday's Child sounded amused. "You went through that, too?"

Caitlin was just glad she couldn't see his face. "And more besides. Why? Didn't you?"

Ashday's Child ignored Caitlin's question. "Come on, Phillip," he said. "What else?"

"We were taught every function of the timepod, and even had complete training simulations."

"And we spent weeks learning about the 1990s," said Nadia. "We were planning on staying for two months, hiring a car, travelling around the UK, staying in hotels, chatting to people. Except that was a waste of time. We should have learned about the 1620s, shouldn't we?"

"Actually, why did you choose the 1990s?" asked Ashday's Child. "That's something that was never made clear in the history files."

"History files? This is our life you're talking about. I suppose you could say then that we're living through history."

"Of course, Nadia. You and Phillip are famous throughout your future history," Ashday's Child said. "Actually, let's just say your names are renowned in certain circles."

"What?"

"Time-travelling circles."

"Oh, I see. All our efforts go unnoticed by the world at large then?"

"Unfortunately so, Phillip. But that's the way it has to be. Time travel is the world's biggest secret. We can't have it for the masses, you know. So, come on, why the 1990s?"

"You must understand it was the first in a series of planned timehops. Once we'd completed that mission we were going to start training to go further back, and then forwards in time.

"But this first one was just to acclimatise us to different cultures and different technology. We didn't want a time in the past where technology was too primitive, or alternatively in our future where *we* would be too primitive. The 1990s were perfect, as that was really the decade of transition, from old technology to new.

"The world was changing fast. The worldwide web was created, and Tim Berners-Lee published the very first website. Newspapers started publishing information online. It was also the time that mobile communications took off. The digital age really began in that era, and it was felt that we should recognise that fact by it being the destination for the very first time travel mission."

"To say nothing of the fact that you wanted to have a go on a PlayStation," said Nadia.

"There is that," admitted Phillip. "I did a thesis at school on the development of both gaming and broadcast technology, as they pretty much ran side by side for a few years, as both utilised the digital revolution. While the 2D graphics of the original PlayStation and televisions are archaic, compared to the holo-image technology that we have today, I was really looking forward to both of those…the console, and watching TV."

"You big kid," said Caitlin. "I'm a thoroughly modern lass when it comes to my pleasures. Only the latest tech for me. I do love going back to olden times, though, such as yours, when I'm working, but I'm always pleased to get home, to civilisation."

"Oi, children, children," said Ashday's Child, before Nadia or Phillip could respond.

*   *   *

The dying world may have been using some strange natural forces to bring its fog from the dark side to the twilight side every five hours, to the exact minute, but there was no telling when the earthquakes would strike within the five-hour period when the fog dominated the terrain. And at the end of it, it would be a different landscape which emerged in the orange light.

So it was this time. A crack ran perilously close to where the travellers clung on to each other as the world shook, danced and reformed around them. But eventually the nightmare ended with the fog trailing back between the mountains as swiftly and mysteriously as it appeared.

Almost as one they breathed a sigh of relief.

"Look at that," whispered Nadia. The crack was within a kilometre of them. They had realised it must be coming close by the ferocity of the land's bucking within that dank, impenetrable blanket. Now they could see it stretching away into the distance, joining many other cracks at the base of a new mountain.

During their journey the topography remained unchanged: just the ground-covering of shale, the canyon-like cracks, jagged mountains, and patches of reeds, all of which were overlooked by that giant, dying orb suspended in the heavens, creating its ethereal orange glow.

A couple of times they had to detour to the end of a canyon that barred their way, but eventually Caitlin told them the Timeshaft should be about a kilometre away. However, she was only getting faint readings from the shuttle.

"So it may not be there, after all," said Nadia, downhearted.

"The readings would normally be stronger than this," Caitlin admitted. "But then again, if the shuttle's waited for us across billions of years, its central core, which would generate the signal, is going to be considerably weakened."

"We'll know soon enough," said Ashday's Child. "But if I were a betting man I'd be backing odds-on that it's there."

Caitlin looked at her watch. "We're not more than a few minutes away, but I don't think we've got time to get there before the fog returns."

Even as she spoke, the dark, thick fibres forming the swirling blanket began to make their way through the mountains from the southwest towards them.

"Here we go again," said Caitlin, keying instructions into the terminal.

With exhaustion, hunger, and thirst now biting at their very core, the travellers were actually looking forward to another period of enforced inactivity, and this time Ashday's Child was persuaded to spend the five hours relating some of his more exciting adventures across the centuries. Even Caitlin was astonished to learn of WorldSave's involvement in certain momentous world events, such as the final disbanding of the European Community in 2059, as well as many unsung happenings.

His stories kept their spirits up and their minds—especially Phillip's—off the fierce battle raging all around them. It was many hours since they had slept, and although they were exhausted and bruised, none of them felt like taking a nap in the fog.

Once again the terminal did its job of keeping the battling hordes at bay beyond the invisible barrier, and eventually the fog swirled away.

Within twenty minutes they reached the site where Caitlin's readings showed the Timeshaft should be.

"Look at this," she said. Shimmering in the air they saw the rounded mouth of the shaft, but nothing could be seen beyond the bluish strands of energy radiating with that familiar electrical buzzing.

"This is the very end of the shaft," mused Ashday's Child. "Proof that existing time is drawing to a close. The matrix responsible for the shaft's existence draws its energy from the ley lines in the living structure of the planet itself. Now the planet's dying there isn't sufficient energy to generate the matrix beyond this point in time, so the shaft finishes here. My theory about us being blasted out of the end was probably right."

"But the energy levels are still tremendously high. So much higher than in the shaft itself," said Caitlin, taking in the information scrolling up the screen. "I don't understand why that should be."

Ashday's Child took the device from her and studied the readout.

"I'll tell you why," he said after a few moments. "The energy's flowing out of the shaft here and dissipating into the earth's atmosphere. These readings aren't of the shaft itself; the energy in the shaft is being overshadowed by this free power as it escapes through the end of the tunnel. That's what we're picking up."

"Is that why the shuttle's readings are so dim?" asked Nadia.

"I don't know," said Ashday's Child. "Let's go into the shaft and see if we've got a ride home or not."

Nadia started to make her way towards the gaping mouth. But Ashday's Child put his hand on her shoulder.

"No. We need to use the portal to be sure of entering the Timeshaft at the precise point where the shuttle should be. The time energy could still mean there's a thousand years or more between the portal and the end of the tunnel."

"But the end of the tunnel's here," protested Nadia.

"Time bears no relation to its immediate space. We could enter the shaft through the end of the tunnel and walk for years before we got to the portal which should be just about here," said Caitlin, firing her watch's ray and looking on with satisfaction as it pushed aside the power flow to create the portal.

Entering the Timeshaft dimension she saw it was the same as in Thiecon. Gone were the gleaming diotanium walls with their concealed lighting system that showed the extent of WorldSave's journeys on regular missions. Instead there were just the raw energy channels, but this time only stretching in one direction: into the past. Either there was no future, or it was unattainable.

But all this was pushed into insignificance by the sight of what lay before them, parked a dozen or so metres along the shaft to the right of the portal.

The timeshuttle.

"I can't believe it," gasped Nadia at the sight of the vessel she had only laid eyes on for a few seconds in the seventeenth century.

"After all these millions of centuries," whispered Phillip, "can it really still be here and fully operational?"

"I hardly dared believe it myself," smiled Caitlin. "But there it is."

"O ye of little faith," said Ashday's Child. "There had to be a way back. Don't forget the circle of time isn't yet complete." He turned to Phillip and Nadia. "You've still got to collect me from the seventeenth century and take me to WorldSave in the twenty-eighth."

"You collected us in the seventeenth," smiled Phillip. "So I suppose it's only fair that we collect you."

Ashday's Child pushed the button on the still gleaming exterior and the door hissed aside. There was a slight whooshing sound as air rushed in to fill the vacuum that, if Caitlin's theory was right, had existed in the timeshuttle for countless centuries, for countless millennia.

"Hmmm. Just a fraction musty," he said, as he stepped inside. Sensing a human presence the computer immediately turned on the heating and lighting to its prearranged settings.

Nestling into the pilot's seat, Ashday's Child brought a dozen basic functions online, but, once more, the time co-ordinates were beyond computable parameters.

"Computer, is all contemporary data held in your memory banks, and is it retrievable?"

"Affirmative," came the commanding female voice. "To compute current millennium will take eight-point-six-two hours. Do you wish computation to commence?"

"No. WorldSave technicians will do that when we get home." He patted the side of the keyboard affectionately. "Which is where we're going right now, old friend. Let's see about powering up your navigation and propulsion systems."

The instant he keyed in the relevant instructions and the computer routed the circuit links through its switching board, the shuttle began to rock gently.

"Computer, what's that?"

"Timeshaft energy is being dispersed into the atmosphere nought-point-one-five kilometres beyond this geographical location. It is flowing past the shuttle. We are now online with the shaft's matrix, meaning—"

"—meaning we're absorbing that wave into our systems. But it's such a gentle movement..." A frown pulled at his forehead as the gauges showing the energy levels barely registered. "Hmmm. According to this we're up to full power, yet the energy conversion is negligible. What's happening?"

"Shuttle's central core has weakened considerably."

"I thought those things lasted forever," muttered Caitlin, leaning against the headrest of his seat.

"'Forever' as we understand the term, yes, they do," replied Ashday's Child. "But this has sat here unused for millions of centuries. That puts an altogether different meaning on 'forever.'"

"But what does it mean for us?" asked Nadia.

"The central core could be described as the shuttle's lungs," he told her. "Most of our power is taken in directly from the living matrix of the Timeshaft itself. The computer's organic link taps into it, drawing in energy. The core then converts that raw energy into usable power to operate the principal systems: in particular, the propulsion unit."

Phillip sank wearily into one of the passenger seats. "So we're still stranded here?" he asked weakly. But it was more of a statement than a question.

Caitlin rested a hand on his shoulder. "Not at all." Suddenly her smile faded. "At least, I hope not. Ashday's Child, the automatic homing unit doesn't rely on the central core, does it?"

"I'm afraid it does," he said. "But there may be a way around it."

"Homing unit?" asked Nadia.

"Yes, there's a homing device built into the shuttle," said Caitlin. "It's intended for use in emergencies to get the shuttle back to our home year of 2745, bypassing all normal control and computer systems."

"But because the central core is supposed to last forever, the homing device's circuits are routed through it," added Ashday's Child.

"Then we *are* stuck here." Nadia sounded vulnerable, defeated. "After all we've come through."

"Well, I don't want to raise any false hopes, but as I said, there may be a way round it," said Ashday's Child. *There has to be; the circle of time isn't yet complete. If we don't somehow get Phillip and Nadia out of here, all this may not happen; WorldSave wouldn't exist, my parents would have died in Thiecon, and I'd never have been born.* The thoughts overrode his fears, curling a smile to his lips. "Yes," he said. "It's got to work. Computer, come offline with the matrix."

He strode out of the shuttle and back through the still open portal into the world beyond. Caitlin, Phillip, and Nadia came up beside him.

"There's our energy source," he said, pointing up to the dying globe hanging listlessly in the gloomy, orange twilight.

"The sun," gasped Phillip. "But how?"

"Solar power was once seen as a viable alternative to artificial forms of energy. If the homing device can be made to bypass the central core and link into a cell harnessing solar power it should boost the system enough to operate the circuits. I think I can rig up a device to tap into the sun's power and store enough for the journey home."

For the next four hours he worked feverishly, alternately at the computer keyboard and ripping out complex control circuits.

"Right," he said eventually, proudly displaying a small black box linked by a cable to the underside of the main control console. "This will store and convert solar power for us."

"But will it be enough to get us home?" asked Caitlin.

"I'm not sure," admitted Ashday's Child. "The computer doesn't know how far ahead of our time we are, so can't compute how much energy the journey will use. But don't worry, because we can easily stop and 'refuel' if we run out." He cocked a thumb skywards. "There'll always be plenty out there."

"It's ironic, isn't it?" said Caitlin quietly. "There's all that power from the Timeshaft flowing past us; power that's probably come from the other end of time itself—from creation—and we can't use it."

Ashday's Child absent-mindedly turned the box around in his hands. "Now all we need is something to catch the sun's power, and we're away."

"There must be enormous power in the shaft," continued Caitlin, not hearing her colleague's musings.

"I think I can convert the computer's intake sensors to do it." Ashday's Child was equally oblivious to what she was saying.

"I remember learning in one of my early WorldSave lectures that there was as much power running through the Timeshaft at any one time as in a two-hundred-billion-megaton nuclear explosion. And it's all going to waste, just flowing through that hole into space."

"If I take the—I beg your pardon?" He whirled away from the control console to face her. "What did you just say?"

"I was saying it's a shame we can't harness all the energy that's going to waste out of the shaft."

"No...the size of the nuclear explosion. What did you say about that?"

"The latent power, at any one point of time and space in the shaft, is equivalent to a two-hundred-billion-megaton nuclear explosion," she recited.

"That's what I thought you said." His voice trailed off. "Is it just possible...?" His eyes shone as he looked at his colleagues with renewed vigour, almost as if he were that young man again, on the threshold of his career with WorldSave fifty years ago. "And I thought it was my destiny to save the world as I knew it. Maybe, just maybe..."

"What is it, what have you thought of?"

"If I can harness enough power from the sun to give to the shuttle, what's to stop me from harnessing power from the Timeshaft and giving it to the sun? A fair exchange, don't you think?"

"But why? Why would you want to do that?"

He gently placed his hands on her shoulders. "Don't you see? A constant bombardment of two hundred billion megatons of energy will rejuvenate the sun. I reckon there's a few thousand years before the sun dies, right...?" His manner, his stance, his words, his face all portrayed the Ashday's Child of old. The eyes were blazing with passion once more. "During those coming years if we can direct enough of that power into it, when the time finally comes and it burns out, a new sun will regenerate.

"Caitlin, don't you understand? We've got the opportunity in our hands to give the world another chance.

"Mankind's died out twice, we know that, and we thought that was it. The end of life on our planet. What we've seen out there, those spiders, those insects, are the only life the dying sun can sustain on Earth."

His words gathered momentum as his eyes shone with visions of the future. A renewed future, made possible by his hand.

"But with a new sun to breathe life into it the earth can live again. Once more there'll be glittering oceans, green hills, forests. It'll be teeming with life. Mankind will have a third chance to evolve. And this time perhaps we won't make the same mistakes as before. Maybe the earth can continue to be beautiful instead of scarred and desecrated in the name of progress. Your civilisation wiped itself out; mine was born from its ashes, but obviously didn't know enough to prevent devastation again. This time it'll be different. And *we*, Caitlin, *we*, can make it happen. We will be the new messiahs."

Caitlin looked at him, dumbstruck. *He's flipped. He's finally flipped.* "We can't create a sun," she insisted. "Look at it out there." She flung an arm towards the shuttle door, towards the open portal out of the Timeshaft where everything was washed in ethereal twilight. "It's dying. We need more than constant power to restart it. The sun generates its energy by nuclear fusion of hydrogen nuclei into helium. The sun, as we knew it in our time, fused 620 million tonnes of hydrogen every second. It's not doing that now, is it? We need nuclear fusion to power it, not just a flow of energy.

"We can't just create a sun," she repeated.

"Why not?" Ashday's Child was on a roll now and not to be stopped. "The power's there, flowing past these very walls. As you said yourself, there's the equivalent of two hundred billion megatons in every point of space and time in the shaft. We've got the equipment in the shuttle to direct that power, and that's all we need, something to focus the power into the sun for the next few thousand years. It really is that simple, Caitlin."

"It is not," she insisted. "Not without the ability to create nuclear fusion. And we don't have the equipment to do that."

"No we don't," he conceded. "We'll just have to hijack it, won't we?"

"What?"

"Hijack it."

"Hijack equipment to create nuclear fusion?"

"Absolutely."

"Here, at the very end of time?"

"Yes." His eyes glazed over for a few seconds as he stared along the Timeshaft looking backwards into the infinity that lay between them and home, recalling his adventure in the Macdonnell mountain range. "I didn't tell you, but something happened when I was with Lloyd Bradman in Australia. Something that shouldn't have happened."

"What?"

"Someone hacked into the operating system of Bradman's solar wind plant. He was concerned that someone was stealing his work. I had to pretend to help find the hacker, or he would've concentrated on that instead of disabling the warning circuits."

He delved deep into the folds of his grimy, grey coat, pulling out an infochip with a flourish reminiscent of a twentieth-century magician producing a rabbit from a hat. "Bradman gave me the access codes to open a route to the hacker. I did load them to open the connection, but didn't do anything else. I was too busy keeping an eye on Bradman.

"I wondered at the time how the hacker could get through the temporal bubble we created, but to be honest I never gave it another thought afterwards, as we went straight on to the TCR case at the Austrian Court. Now I know why the hacker was able to get through. I'm the hacker."

Caitlin shook her head. "I'm sorry, but you've lost me completely."

"Me too," said Phillip. "I've been listening to the conversation without understanding a word of it."

"Bradman's dream was to harness the power of solar wind, a highly unstable stream of charged particles originating in the sun's corona: an original product of nuclear fusion.

"Within the confines of that time bubble I opened the link directly to the hacker. All I need do now is access the bubble's co-ordinates, 4:11 and fifteen seconds on July 30, 2345, use Bradman's codes on this infochip to open the link to his system there, and download his solar wind data. This will give me all the information I need to calibrate this somewhat-cobbled-together equipment. Firing solar wind back into the sun in the same power stream as the energy from the Timeshaft will kick-start the nuclear fusion we need to begin the regeneration process."

Caitlin stared at her mentor in disbelief.

If he'd worked feverishly before during the four hours it took to build the solar energy converter to power the timeshuttle's central core, he worked like a whirling dervish now, and continuing unabated for eighteen hours, ignoring his colleagues' protests that they needed food.

Their last meal had been breakfast with the Earl of Berkeley in the seventeenth century, and despite the fact that the timeshuttle was hermetically sealed during its wait through eternity, the on-board food supply was an inevitable victim.

Ahead of the next period of fog, Caitlin closed the portal linking the shaft's dimension to the harsh outside world. But before she did, she, Phillip and Nadia couldn't resist standing at the high-energy blue-tinged matrix lines looking out as the swirling, greasy tendrils swung in to take possession of the lands beyond, slowly thickening into a stranglehold. And all the time Ashday's Child sat in the shuttle, dismantling seemingly endless amounts of equipment.

"I sure hope he knows what he's doing," said Phillip, glancing back through the open door.

"If anyone can succeed in this crazy plan, it's Ashday's Child. He's our best operative," said Caitlin.

At one stage he joined them briefly, when he emerged from the shuttle and laid down his black box, which now sported a concave dish. "To attract the sun's rays," he told them. A cable connected the dish to the box, and when he switched the device on, a digital readout began its slow ascent.

"When it reaches one hundred units it'll be full, and we can see about leaving here. Now, all I need do is combine the shaft's power with the solar wind and focus it into the sun."

When Ashday's Child returned to the shuttle, Phillip looked back down the Timeshaft, then closely at the blue-tinged matrix lines. "All this power," he mused. "It doesn't seem possible."

"It is, though," said Caitlin. "I know it's hard to believe, but there really is the equivalent energy of a two-hundred-billion-megaton nuclear explosion in every single atom of space and every single microsecond of time in the entire length of the shaft. Right from the beginning of time, through to the very end, here."

"And he's going to blast it all into the sun."

Hours later, with stomachs rumbling, they finally helped him carry one of the shuttle's display touchscreens linked to a data storage drive, and what looked like half the shuttle's circuitry and navigation system, to the edge of the Timeshaft's wall. He then disappeared back inside the shuttle, returning a couple of moments later with a large saucer-shaped panel, into which was linked every output channel the craft contained, along with every other directional object on board, including the fire extinguishers, torches, and all laser tubes.

"Now," he said, squatting down to the touchscreen. "Let's get this set up." As his fingers played across the screen, the saucer-shaped panel turned fractionally until its tubular extrusions were pointing straight at the fading sun.

With a nod of evident pride he looked at the data flowing across the screen. "On target. All that remains to do now, is…" He jabbed at a couple of the icons, and the readout changed instantly.

"Look at this," he said, indicating one of three rows of rising columns. "This shows the amount of power being directed through the equipment. While this…" he pointed to the middle column, "…indicates its speed and direction. And this third one is the program to keep it locked on to the sun.

"This, my friends, is going to create our new world for us."

A few moments later he retrieved the black box and connected it to what was left of the on-board computer. And a few moments after that, the shuttle's door hissed shut.

"I've never used the homing system," he told them, strapping himself into the pilot's seat. "It could be rough, it could be smooth. Let's see, shall we?"

He hit a sequence of keys, watching with satisfaction as the instruments reflected computer predictions.

"Yes, the system's powering up nicely. It is. Any minute now we should be on our way."

A green light to one side of the console came on, and Ashday's Child hit the final execute key. With only the tiniest of shudders and the barest increase in humming, the shuttle left the end of time, on its way back through eternity.

* * *

And it came to pass that two thousand years after a man known as Ashday's Child arrived at the end of the world, proclaiming himself to be the new messiah, the sun of that small, insignificant solar system reached the end of its natural existence. For billions upon billions of millennia it had lived, extending its life-giving heat and light to its children—hunks of rock spinning endlessly around it. For the merest blink of an eye one of those planets had sported human life. But the species destroyed itself, only to rise from the ashes for a second chance. Even that civilisation failed. And now the world itself had died.

The blistering, immeasurable heat of the explosion ninety-three million miles away across the blackness of space, scorched the earth. In an instant the only remaining life forms—insects and spiders— were wiped out. The temperature at the very core of the planet rose a billion-billion-billionfold. The rocks heaved. The land became molten. The entire planet became a blistering sphere of bubbling decay.

And in the heavens, a small yellow sun created by Ashday's Child, looked down on the children of its father.

Children with another chance.

CHAPTER 12

CLOSING CIRCLES

SLEEP, AFTER ALL THEY HAD BEEN THROUGH during the last couple of days, was their immediate priority on the interminable journey back through the ages. It also provided a blessed relief against the pangs of hunger coursing through their bodies. The girls used the tiny rooms at the back of the speeding craft, while Phillip spread himself out on the floor in the living quarters. Ashday's Child catnapped in the pilot's seat after leaving instructions for the computer to wake him in the event of any change, however small, to their flight path.

As his eyes flickered open between each fitful doze, his gaze went straight to the chronometer, which showed several times that the vessel was still travelling beyond computed parameters. Finally, it registered the year 4973. They were back into charted territory.

The computer told him that at their current velocity—and because they were using the homing device there was no way of varying it—the rest of their journey would take just over seven hours. He sank into a more comfortable sleep, secure in the knowledge that if they did have to stop to "refuel" from the sun, there would at least be some sort of civilisation beyond the confines of the Timeshaft, not an unknown, derelict land providing life only to hostile creatures.

With two hours to go before the shuttle was due to dock at Landing Bay Seven, Ashday's Child opened video communications with WorldSave HQ and asked to speak to Dr. Bob Gannaton.

"That's twice in two days you've done this to me," protested Dr Gannaton, good-naturedly.

"Done what?" Ashday's Child was genuinely mystified.

"What happened to your shuttle? It suddenly vanished off our monitoring systems in the seventeenth century. One moment it was there, the next, gone. And then a few hours ago we picked you up on the homing frequency coming in from the fiftieth century. But you didn't answer our hailing signals."

"We didn't hear you. I've had to dismantle the frequency monitor. I needed it to watch over the Timeshaft's frequency range for a few thousand years."

Dr. Gannaton frowned. "I beg your pardon?"

Ashday's Child also frowned, dismissing his chief executive's amazement, trying to get a handle on what appeared to be another time paradox. *What happened to the shuttle? As it had waited for us through eternity it should have continued to show up in the shaft. Shouldn't it? But then again, if that were the case, now we're on our way back, the shuttle will pass through all those moments of "real time" which prevailed in the shaft. And that means it would co-exist in the shaft at the same time as the stationary one waiting for us.*

"I'll tell you all about it when we get home," he replied. "We've got Phillip Oatridge and Nadia Reeder on board, and I think we need to conduct some urgent business with them when we arrive. Could you book the conference room, please, and join us for a couple of hours when we get back?"

Dr. Gannaton smiled, as if he'd been about suggest the same thing. "Of course. But what's this all about?"

Ignoring the chief executive's question, Ashday's Child continued: "Have our technicians finished upgrading TRAEP's pod?"

"Yes, they've been back for hours. Everything went fine. Temporal stabilisers have been fitted, so it's not going to damage the shaft anymore."

"Good. Look, Bob, I've got a favour to ask. Could someone retrieve the pod for me, please? I'd like it to be there when Nadia and Phillip arrive. I need them to make a couple of time trips for me on their way back home."

Dr. Gannaton stared for a moment at the lined, ugly features looking back at him from the screen. But the weasel eyes gave nothing away. In fact they glinted somewhat mischievously. "Okay," he said, eventually. "But I want a full explanation from you."

"And you'll get one, don't worry. Oh, and Bob, two more things. We haven't eaten since the seventeenth century, which was at least two days ago. Can you lay on some food for us in the anteroom, please? And can you pull file AC2067 from my computer—the file password is 'Resign.' It's for you, and that's exactly what it is. My resignation."

And with that bombshell, Ashday's Child cut the connection, smiling at the thought of Dr. Gannaton trying unsuccessfully to re-establish contact. The shuttle's only system for recognising an incoming call was at the end of time, regulating the flow of power into the sun.

He leaned back in the seat, instantly falling into a deep and contented sleep.

* * *

"Shuttle will dock in precisely ten minutes," announced the computer, breaking into his slumber.

He pulled himself up and glanced across the instrumentation panels. The solar power had lasted their journey out; according to the readout there was still enough to keep them going for another hour.

Better wake the others, he said to himself. *I have a feeling Bob himself will be among our welcoming committee.*

It wasn't long before Ashday's Child powered down the systems and the shuttle door hissed aside. The landing bay was one of eight in a vast cathedral-like chamber on a ley line in the Timeshaft dimension at WorldSave's headquarters in the remote Highlands of New Scotland.

Ashday's Child opened a compartment concealed in the underside of the control console and pulled out two data storage keys—one green, one blue—which he slotted away inside the folds of his grimy coat, before standing up and making his way towards the door.

The welcoming committee consisted of just one person. And he had been right. It was Bob Gannaton.

"Ah, Bob," said Ashday's Child, striding confidently from the craft. "Let me introduce Phillip Oatridge and Nadia Reeder, the world's first time travellers. Without whom none of WorldSave's activities would be possible."

Phillip and Nadia barely blinked. Although they had only known Ashday's Child for a couple of days they had already come to expect the unexpected from him.

Dr. Gannaton led the way from the Timeshaft to an elevator which took them to the top of floor of WorldSave House, and into a room with stunning, unspoilt views over the northern tip of Loch Shin.

"Thank goodness some things never change," marvelled Nadia, staring out of the window. "Where are we now? 2745?"

Dr Gannaton nodded.

"I was here at Loch Shin on holiday in 2562, just before starting my Astro-Temporal Physics course," said Nadia.

Ashday's Child smiled. "Then you may be interested to know that in 2685 I was responsible for preventing this area from becoming a nuclear dumping ground. A timeline projection showed that without WorldSave intervention a broken seal on a canister buried a mile underground would have led to radiation contamination of the whole of Northern Scotland within ten years. The area you see now would be nothing but desolate wilderness."

"The world has a lot to thank you for, Ashday's Child," said Phillip.

"The world has a lot to thank *you* for, as well," he replied. "Without the cycle of events which you began when your pod damaged the Timeshaft I don't believe any of this would have been possible."

Dr. Gannaton looked at Ashday's Child in amazement. He thought he had become immune to the agent's surprises, but this one managed to smash that illusion to pieces.

"And that circle is now closing," continued Ashday's Child, pulling the two data keys from his pocket and sliding the green one into the access portal of the wall-based computer. He took a smoked salmon sandwich from the food display on the central table and sat back.

"This first key," he said, looking first at Phillip, then at Nadia, "is for the directors of TRAEP. Not the people you've been working with, but those who came before. I want you to use your timepod to go back ten years before your inaugural mission. You left in 2566, right? I'd like you to go to 2556 and give this key to a gentleman named Professor Simon Lindquist."

"TRAEP's founder."

"Exactly, Nadia. It contains certain information to help the fledgling organisation with its time experiments. Without it time travel would never get off the ground."

"But this key must contain flawed information," protested Dr. Gannaton. "We've got the opportunity to give them the right information so their inaugural flight won't damage the Timeshaft."

"Bob," smiled Ashday's Child indulgently. "They *have* to damage the shaft, otherwise I'd never be sent to rescue them, which means I'd never bring my parents to the seventeenth century—my parents would die in their own time before I was born. If I'm not born the Timeshaft is never discovered, maybe not even created. It's all part of the time paradox—the time circle—that TRAEP's maiden voyage does indeed damage the Timeshaft in this way."

"Sorry, Ashday's Child," said Dr. Gannaton. "You've completely lost me."

"It'll become clearer. I hope." He turned again to Phillip and Nadia. "This key gives TRAEP's scientists a foothold on the time travel ladder and paves the way for the merging of TRAEP and WorldSave in 2692, which is the year I arrived at WorldSave with the key that *you* gave *me*." He held the other key aloft. "We'll have a look at this in a moment. Meanwhile, let's just play the introduction of this one, which you're taking to Professor Lindquist."

He thumbed a button on the handheld remote, and a half-metre-high 3D image of himself sprang to life in the centre of the table.

"Greetings, Professor Lindquist," said the hologram. "I am known as Ashday's Child, and this key contains the secrets of time travel which I believe you are currently striving for.

"How do I know this?" The image smiled enigmatically.

That same smile, noted Caitlin, *the one I've seen a hundred times during the last few weeks.*

"I come from your future, from the year 2692 to be precise, when time travel is on the brink of being used for the benefit of mankind. But without your experiments, successful time travel will remain an impossible dream.

"The information you're about to be given will help you create a timepod, enabling a crew of two to travel backwards and forwards in time. It's essential for the success of your mission that you recruit a certain young couple as pilots for the first voyage. TRAEP will be ready to make that voyage in the year 2566. Two years before that you will seek out Dr. Ferdinand Russell, Principal of the Central Academy of Greater England, and sponsor the final eighteenth months of a four-year Astro-Temporal Physics course being undertaken by Phillip Oatridge and Nadia Reeder. They will be your pilots.

"Remember, Professor Lindquist, the success of time travel depends on your carrying out these instructions to the letter—as indeed, does the very existence of mankind."

The holographic projection of Ashday's Child vanished, to be replaced by another image. But Ashday's Child snapped a button on the remote unit, dissolving the figure.

"I think that's all we need to see of that," he said, pulling the key from the drive and replacing it with the other one.

"This is the key you have to give me when you meet me in the seventeenth century on my twentieth birthday."

The touch of another button brought the same hologram of Ashday's Child shimmering into existence again at the centre of the table.

"Hi, Ashday's Child," began the figure. "If Phillip and Nadia have carried out my request"—The figure glanced at the precise spot where they now sat, as if it knew exactly where they would be—"and I'm sure you have"—the image looked straight ahead again—"you'll be seeing this for the first time aboard their timepod on your twentieth birthday. You'll see it many more times when you arrive at your destination in 2692, and on those occasions you can bypass this introduction. But for now, please listen carefully.

"I'm...well, you know who I am as you see me every time you look in a mirror, don't you? Except I'm about fifty years older now— but I think you can still see me in you, can't you? Your parents will have already told you that you come from a civilisation centuries into the future. But what they haven't told you is that it's your destiny to bring the secret of time travel to the world, enabling an environmental campaigning organisation called WorldSave to travel through the ages, putting right the mess mankind tries to make of the environment.

"I want you to seek out Michael Heilbron, the chief executive of WorldSave, and give him this data key. It contains details of a living entity called the Timeshaft, which connects the ages, starting in prehistoric times and running, as far as we know, right to the very end of time itself.

"By utilising this key, WorldSave will be able to access the Timeshaft—in fact, the wristwatch you're wearing now opens portals leading from the Timeshaft to any era you choose.

"WorldSave technicians will be able to build shuttle vehicles, giving agents the means to travel the vast distances through time relatively quickly.

"One last thing before I suggest you hand this key over to Michael Heilbron: it's you who take your own parents from the land of Thiecon in the far future, to the seventeenth century where you're born. This will occur during the time you're called upon to rescue Phillip Oatridge and Nadia Reeder from that same era.

"When that task is complete, and only then, can you rest, Ashday's Child. Your destiny will have been faced."

He hit the remote, dissolving the image.

"Well," said Dr. Gannaton. "You've kept that quiet all these years."

"Yes, I'm sorry about that." Ashday's Child looked uncharacteristically sheepish. "I felt no-one else should ever know the truth until the mission was accomplished. It would create too many variables, and goodness knows there were enough of those already."

He retrieved the key from its slot, handing them both to Phillip. As Phillip took them, a shudder visibly shook the older man. "There goes my destiny," he smiled. "My task's complete. It's up to you now."

Ashday's Child stood up and ambled wearily across to the window, absorbing the breathtaking view across Loch Shin. "That very key, telling me about myself and giving WorldSave details of the Timeshaft, is the actual one given to me by Phillip and Nadia when they collected me on my twentieth birthday. I've kept it all these years."

He turned back to face the young couple. "And I now pass it to you to give to me when you collect me." He handed the key across to Phillip.

"As to the other one… You, Phillip, also brought that with you in your timepod. There's an instruction on it for you to take it on

TRAEP's first voyage and give it to a character called Ashday's Child. But according to the information on the key, that meeting is supposed to take place in the twentieth century."

"So something went wrong in this great time paradox," said Caitlin.

"I don't think so," replied Ashday's Child. "I think it was intended that the pod should attempt to land in the twentieth century so it could rip that hole in the shaft's matrix down to the seventeenth. Don't forget that without that rip Phillip and Nadia would never have been stranded there, and we'd never have needed to rescue them.

"All I know is that everything appears to have happened as it's laid down in those two data keys. All that remains to be done now is for Phillip and Nadia to deliver them safely."

"One thing's still puzzling me," said Dr. Gannaton. "How did you know all the technical details about the Timeshaft?"

"Ah," said Ashday's Child. "There is just one more thing about that."

"There always is with you."

"In my own personal timeline I haven't recorded those data keys yet."

"What?"

"Just another little paradox, I think."

"You are...infuriating at times."

"Explanations, you always want explanations. Phillip, could I borrow the first key for a moment, please?"

Mystified, Phillip handed the green key back to Ashday's Child, who slotted it into the computer portal and accessed the spot where he switched it off before.

"Professor Lindquist," began the newly materialised computer-generated figure. "Good day. I'm Leon Abrinsky. I'm a time technician, and the information I'm about to give you will help you construct your first timepod. The age of time travel on the earth has reached its dawn."

Dr. Gannaton leapt up. "Turn it off," he shouted.

Ashday's Child complied, and looked expectantly at his boss.

"You've taken one liberty too much with that. You had no right asking a time technician to record that without my permission."

"Bob, Bob, he hasn't recorded it. As I said a moment ago, in my personal timeline I haven't said any of this yet."

Gannaton looked blank. "But it's here. We've seen it. We've heard it."

"Yes. And if Leon and I don't record it, what do you think's going to happen?"

"I don't have a clue, but I'm sure you're going to enlighten us."

"Hardly," said Ashday's Child. "For the simple reason that I don't have a clue either. But we have to make these recordings now, before we take Phillip and Nadia back to their timepod and see them safely on their way. The possible consequences to the timeline are too horrific to contemplate, if we don't. Ever since Phillip gave me these two keys on my twentieth birthday, in the seventeenth century, I've been waiting for this moment, and I'm not going to risk anything now.

"I've got a full transcript of both keys in my room. While I fetch it, Bob, perhaps you could ask Leon Abrinsky to join us. He's got a lot of information to record for Professor Simon Lindquist and a fair few detailed time engineering files to download."

*   *   *

The next morning Ashday's Child was woken by the buzzing of the bedside communicator in his living quarters on the third floor at WorldSave.

"Sorry to disturb you so early," said Dr. Gannaton. "But I thought you might like to hear what we've discovered from the computer's databanks on board your shuttle."

"What is it?" Ashday's Child hauled himself up on one elbow.

"Can you come to my office? I'm getting Caitlin here, too."

"Sure. Give me ten minutes."

Caitlin was already there when he arrived at Dr. Gannaton's penthouse office.

"What's this all about?"

"Our technicians have been analysing the data stored in your computer, from the time the shuttle left here on your last mission." Dr. Gannaton tapped a button on his desk console, bringing a screen to life, which was scrolling a mass of information.

"This is the relevant part," he said, hitting a key to stop the flow of information, and another to blank the screen. "Just before we examine it, can you tell me again where Thiecon is and why you had to go there?"

"Well, it's my parents' original home. They were going to be executed because I'd have been born in a period of the year called Ashday, when it's forbidden to have children. But you know this already." He looked puzzled. There was something a tad unsettling in Dr. Gannaton's expression.

"Let me rephrase the question. Rather than where is it, *when* is it?"

"I don't know. All I know is that it's at some point in the far future, after mankind wipes himself out. My civilisation grows from the ashes of this one."

Dr. Gannaton nodded solemnly. "So you'd led us to believe."

Ashday's Child sat bolt upright. "What do you mean by that?"

"Is that what you genuinely think?"

"Of course it is. What are you getting at?"

"Take a look at this." Dr Gannaton brought life back to the screen. "Your computer shows that after the braking process to stop your flight into the far future when you were caught in the temporal wave, your reverse journey took you far beyond this current era, and back in time. Way, way back in time."

Ashday's Child stared at the screen, blankly.

"Your shuttle stopped for a brief period in what's always been known as the Triassic Age, approximately 225 million years ago. There's no doubt about it…" He leaned forward and gently touched Ashday's Child's arm. "That's when you picked up your parents.

"It wasn't our civilisation that destroyed itself, with yours rising from those ashes. It was your civilisation which wiped itself out; ours grew after yours."

Recoiling in horror, Ashday's Child slumped back in his seat. Caitlin reached across and took hold of his hand.

His head spun. The room around him faded, became indistinct to his numbed senses. Everything he believed in, everything he held dear, had suddenly been shattered by the evidence on the computer screen.

Dimly he recalled stories his father told him, stories originally related to the people of Thiecon by the Holy Man and Star-Gazer. Stories of how Mankind had wiped Himself out and how Thiecon was built from that devastation. Why, the very curse of an Ashday's Child was spawned from the destruction of the old world.

He looked starkly around the room. "Then that makes you, this civilisation, the third to walk upon the earth," he said softly.

Dr. Gannaton could see the devastating effect it was having on Ashday's Child. "It changes our history, too," he said. "We need to rethink everything."

"Unless the Star-Gazer's words weren't recounting the past." Ashday's Child looked down at his hands. "Maybe his account of a reclaimed world, built again after a mechanised age, was a prophecy, speaking of a catastrophe which at that time hadn't happened, but was still to come."

CHAPTER 13

NEW DESTINIES

ASHDAY'S CHILD held a bag containing his personal possessions from the now stripped and unusable timeshuttle, along with essential computer records from its databanks, and stepped out of his beloved craft one last time.

He paused to shut the door and strode away without a backward glance. He had come to love that sleek, bullet-shaped vessel which had carried him beyond eternity—in *both* directions it seemed now.

How long would it take, he wondered, to come to terms with the fact that the world he had spent his entire life saving was the one which grew up from the ruins of his own civilisation? And all these years he had felt smug in the belief that he was the saviour from the far future, come back in time to teach these heathens how to look after their world a little longer. Now it turned out the people of his civilisation were the heathens; they were the ones who destroyed themselves. His philosophy was built upon shifting sands.

But why were there no records of this ancient civilisation? Had the catastrophe been so immense that it managed to wipe out every trace of its very existence? His recollection of geological time told him that the Triassic Age was about halfway along the scale, just before the Jurassic Age, when supposedly, dinosaurs ruled the earth. Had his people been replaced as custodians of the earth by creatures with brains the size of a pea? He had to know the truth.

There were three more shuttles currently at home base, and purely at random he chose the one in Landing Bay Four. The door hissed open in response to his touch on the recessed control on the gleaming wall. As he stepped inside, the computer turned on the lights and brought life support out of hibernation. He looked around. An absolute copy of his own shuttle. No problems here.

Dropping his bag onto the compact table in the living quarters he settled down in the pilot's seat. There would be time enough for finding a home for the small number of things he owned when he was underway. Likewise, for storing computer information from his own shuttle in this one's memory circuits. But there was one set of data which had to be loaded now. The time data giving details of his previous voyage to Thiecon. He slotted the key into the drive unit and set co-ordinates for 230 million years in the past.

Powering up the systems, he noticed with satisfaction that the ever-present background hum was less noticeable than on his own craft and the lights didn't adopt their customary process of dimming just ever so slightly as the main propulsion and navigation circuits cut in.

"Hmmm, a newer model. I'm going to enjoy this," he said, then checked the clasp on his new wristwatch, purloined from central stores.

The shuttle glided smoothly out of Landing Bay Four, connected with the main Timeshaft and started its long journey back through the ages, back through eternity.

And inside, Ashday's Child slept, dreaming of new destinies.

*   *   *

In that dream, Ashday's Child saw fog hanging low over the dying lands. A fog far removed from the shimmering white mist once seen above fields and water in the moments after dawn. On this tainted world, dawns had long since ceased to exist. So had sunsets, so had days, and so had nights.

All that remained for countless millennia was a heavy, foreboding twilight, as the once-beautiful green jewel of the cosmos lay locked on its axis, hurtling around the brand new yellow sun which was just beginning to flood the plains of derelict, scorched terrain with renewed, life-giving forces.

Time in this part of the Matrix of Creation had been drawing to a close. There were many yesterdays—billions upon billions of them—and now, with an unexpected, shining new star in the heavens, there were also billions upon billions of precious tomorrows.

Mankind's mastery of the planet had been but a fleeting moment of triumph. The poison which mankind put into his kingdom performed its deadly work. The world had become tired and diseased while still in its infancy and long before the sun grew old and weary it was nothing but a stinking, choking hell-hole.

Thick contaminated slime, which had once formed the dazzling, crystal oceans, seeped and oozed its way over the decaying land, hastening its dereliction.

And then fog claimed the planet. A fog which was rusty brown, moody, and oppressive. But which was becoming less so with each successive five-hour cycle.

What had once been a dim red twilight, was now becoming a wondrous new dawn of pure, golden sunlight beaming across the immensity of space, giving hope for a new beginning.

Hope for a new civilisation.

THE END

EXTRACT FROM STEWART BINT'S

IN SHADOWS WAITING

Published by Booktrope, August 2015

The creature's triumphant laugh would stay with me until my dying day. Something I never wanted to hear again.

It was the strongest memory to stir as I looked at the photo, the colours of which had dimmed with age. Thirty-two years ago it had been vibrant and full of life. Just like the faces staring back at me from the time before shadows. From the time before torment. From the time when we were happy.

It all reminded me of when the world was young and innocent— hell, when *I* was young and innocent. My two daughters both started sleeping with their boyfriends as soon as they turned sixteen, probably before then, if the truth were told. If they had, it was something both they and my wife kept from me. But it was a different era when my sisters were that age. Helen and her Mark. Sarah and the succession of boyfriends she brought to our home, White Pastures.

I rarely smile now. Even after thirty-two years, the memories were painful. Fifty now. A half century. I was eighteen then. Yet in some ways it still seems like only yesterday.

Time plays tricks.

A tear rolls down my cheek.

ABOUT THE AUTHOR

Stewart Bint is a novelist, magazine columnist and PR writer. He lives with his wife, Sue, in Leicestershire in the UK, and has two grown-up children, Christopher and Charlotte.

While writing, his office companion is his charismatic budgie, Alfie, or his neighbour's cat. But not at the same time.

When not writing he can often be found hiking barefoot on woodland trails.

CONNECT WITH STEWART BINT ONLINE:

Website:

www.stewartbintauthor.weebly.com

Blog:

www.Stewartbintauthor.weebly.com/stewart-bints-blog

Twitter:

twitter.com/@AuthorSJB

Facebook:

https://www.facebook.com/StewartBintAuthor

MORE GREAT READS FROM BOOKTROPE

A Beginner's Guide to Invading Earth by **Gerhard Gehrke** (Science Fiction) Jeff, an ex-computer programmer, framed for the deaths of aliens, battles the odds to clear his name and find the true culprits behind the multiple dead alien bodies.

A Memory in the Black by **Michael G. Munz** (Science Fiction) As a conspiracy to save humanity from itself struggles to unlock the secrets of the alien spacecraft known as Paragon, others plot to seize it for themselves. Now Diomedes has assassinated a man at the heart of Paragon's discovery. Can Michael Flynn and Marc Triton survive long enough to learn why?

Alien Love by **Stan Schatt** (Science Fiction) When the woman he loves turns out to be an alien with her own agenda, an ex-SEAL must race against extraterrestrials far stronger and far more cunning than any human enemy. Casablanca meets Star Wars

Cathedral of Dreams by **Terry Persun** (Science Fiction) A compelling tale of a dystopian future and personal heroism, pitting the outsiders against the mind-control machine of New City.

Daimones by **Massimo Marino** (Science Fiction) Nothing could have prepared them for the last day. Explore the future of humanity in this apocalyptic tale that feels like it could happen tomorrow.

EXODUS 2022 by **Kenneth G. Bennett** (Science Fiction) A young man discovers that the hallucination destroying his mind holds clues to a looming global calamity.

Ouroboros by **Christopher Turkel** (Science Fiction) In a dystopian future, Thomas the assassin is about to face the job of his career—and his life.

Sugar Scars by **Travis Norwood** (Science Fiction) A nineteen-year-old type 1 diabetic survives the apocalypse and realizes that insulin expires. She needs to find a way to make it herself or die.

Would you like to read more books like these?
Subscribe to **runawaygoodness.com**, get a free ebook for signing up, and never pay full price for an ebook again.

Lightning Source UK Ltd.
Milton Keynes UK
UKOW02f1947130416

272152UK00004B/123/P